CUT-PRICE LAWMAN

They wanted a sheriff they could control and run the town their way ... then along came Chris Cade: a drifter, drunk, stupid with toothache and broke. The badge was easy to pin on him. But Cade, with his own agenda and rules, had a pair of hard fists and a fast gun. They figured they'd got him for a cut-rate, but the price they paid put them deep in the red — and the well-turned soil of Boot Hill.

TYLER HATCH

◆

CUT-PRICE LAWMAN

Complete and Unabridged

LINFORD
Leicester

First published in Great Britain in 2011 by
Robert Hale Limited
London

First Linford Edition
published 2013
by arrangement with
Robert Hale Limited
London

British Library CIP Data

Hatch, Tyler.
  Cut-price lawman. - -
  (Linford western library)
  1. Western stories.
  2. Large type books.
  I. Title II. Series
  823.9'2–dc23

  ISBN 978–1–4448–1489–7

Published by
F. A. Thorpe (Publishing)
Anstey, Leicestershire

Set by Words & Graphics Ltd.
Anstey, Leicestershire
Printed and bound in Great Britain by
T. J. International Ltd., Padstow, Cornwall

This book is printed on acid-free paper

1

Reno Creek

Chris Cade was tall, lean, over thirty, and hard-muscled, as tough as any range-rider west of the Mississippi — maybe a good deal tougher than many.

He had faced yelling, painted Indians, hardcases' blazing guns, forest fires, flooded rivers, ridden down stampeding herds, fought with fists, boots and guns as the occasion arose, *but* ... when it came to facing a frontier dentist, he discovered he had a yellow streak, shoulder-wide and belly deep.

The molar on the left side of his badly swollen jaw had been troubling him for over a week now — and he hadn't been entirely sober for more than a few hours during that time. He had tried a heap of remedies to kill the pain of the crumbling tooth: Indian herbs worked for a spell — a very *short* spell; he packed gunpowder into the cavity, but all that did was give him a filthy taste in a mouth that seemed choked with lightning bolts; he chewed cloves and chilli-peppers — and they gave a little relief but burned the inside of his cheek: he figured he had enough pain without adding to it.

There was all kinds of muck that well-meaning sidekicks, sometimes with a twisted sense of humour, suggested as a remedy, but deep down he knew the only real answer to the problem was to square up and have the tooth yanked.

He reached his decision when he emptied yet another bottle of whiskey he had nurtured on his two day ride up to Reno Creek. But when he entered the town, swaying in the saddle, half-awake, brain fogged with whiskey fumes, he began to weaken: he tried to fight it — really hard.

No, goddamnit! That tooth's gotta come out!

Crossing the entrance to a side street running off Main, he slowed his smoke gelding, squinting to read a shingle he saw swinging on a rusted iron bracket over an archway leading to a flight of stairs running up the side of a clapboard building.

PAINLESS DENTIST
Only Latest Humane Gas used
Guaranteed — No Pain
Or No Charge

That sounded OK: but Cade didn't like the idea much of being put to sleep, especially with some strange gas — anyway, his finances were close to hitting rock bottom.

'Reckon I've got enough for a double shot of red eye — *just to see me through*,' he told himself, and turned the smoke towards the hitchrail outside the nearest saloon.

Even dismounting in slow motion sent pain surging through his jaw and neck and ear to crash against the top of his skull. The intensity of it blurred his vision and he grasped the saddlehorn until the spasm passed, then stumbled his way across the boardwalk towards the batwings.

He weaved drunkenly, from fatigue and the strength-sapping pain as well as the amount of liquor he had consumed. As he started through the batwings a big man arrived at the same point from inside the saloon and, red-eyed, unshaven, reeking of booze, shouted over his shoulder, presumably at the barkeep:

'You get ridda that bitch, Burl, or I'll do it for you!'

'Won't have my gals slapped around by the customers, Casey. You know that.'

'Know I'll be back — an' you better watch out when I am ... whether you're still holdin' that sawn-off or not.'

The man slammed the batwings one-handed and the edge caught Cade's elbow as he held a hand to his throbbing jaw. The pain made him almost scream, as the impact jarred along his arm and transferred to his hand, driving it hard against his swollen jaw.

He roared a curse as the big man, startled to find Cade in front of him, suddenly snarled and shoved the cowboy violently aside. 'Outta my way, stumblebum!'

Cade crashed against the wall and the swinging batwing caught him in the chest as Casey bulled through.

Cade hit his head against the wall when the batwing slammed him back and through a red haze of agony and fury saw Casey barging past on to the saloon porch. Boiling anger engulfed him.

'*Hey!*' Cade yelled, the effort hurting his jaw even more as he reached for the thick arm closest to him. He dug in his fingers and swung Casey about, catching the man in mid-step so that he stumbled.

Casey's red, unshaven face deepened in colour and he curled a lip as he stepped back towards Cade, towering over the cowboy now hunched over with the griping throb that seemed to consume his entire body. He was actually six feet two inches tall but right now looked a lot smaller.

Casey balled a big fist, ready to knock Cade's head off his shoulders. One glimpse and Chris Cade erupted like a volcano, focusing his rage fully on the bigger man. Without hesitation he pulled his Colt from leather and the sunlight flashed and winked from the barrel as it whipped back and forth across Casey's startled face, cracking down across the front of his skull. Skin split and blood spurted as the big man went down in a kind of wavering corkscrew, his legs crossed as they gave way beneath him. His battered, blood-streaked face smashed into the doorframe, bounced off, and Casey spread out, unmoving.

Cade straightened slowly, leathering the gun, blinking. The drinkers stared, most gap-mouthed, and the barkeep looked up slowly from Casey's inert form, laying down the sawn-off shotgun he had been holding on the counter.

'Judas, mister! You just earned yourself a slew of drinks on the house!' He looked around, grinning at the audience. 'None of us never figured we'd ever see that goddamn bully laid out like that! Right, boys?'

Murmuring from the crowd grew louder as many agreed with the 'keep. Two men grabbed the swaying Cade by the arms as he tried to nurse his face, but jumped back when he snarled at them. One man lifted his arms hastily, palms out as he started to back off.

'Hey, hey, *hey*, friend! We — we just wanna buy you a drink . . . '

The friendly tone seeped through to Cade's thudding brain and he nodded, gasped: 'S-sorry — Goddamn toothache.'

'Got just the thing for it!' The barkeep reached under the counter, brought out a dark green squat bottle and sloshed some brownish liquid into the bottom half of a beer glass. He pushed it along the bar towards Cade, seeing now the lopsided face as the man grimaced in his suffering.

Cade grabbed the glass in both hands and gulped it down, afterwards opening his mouth as wide as the puffed skin would allow, gasping for breath.

'Christ, man! You're meant to rinse and spit! Not swallow!'

Cade glared, gagging, in a sick, filthy mood now.

'Jeeeesusssss . . . What is that stuff?'

The barkeep straightened his face. '*Amigo*, I gotta tell you — it ain't gonna fix that toothache. You better go see Doc Payne. They say the new gas he's got really works.'

'*Payne*! A dentist named *Payne*!'

'Yeah, hell ain't it? But listen, I wouldn't steer you wrong. He's good. Costs a bit . . . '

'Lets me out,' Cade said quickly and couldn't keep the great relief from his voice. 'I'm about broke.'

The barman and saloon owner, Burl

Randall, looked around at the gawking customers. Casey was still lying in his own blood unmoving, beneath the batwings. 'What d'ya say, gents? Worth kickin' in a little, just to've seen Casey brought down to the common denominator . . . ?'

There was a roar of agreement and Cade looked more pained than ever as the money was piled on the bar top. *Damn!* Now there was no excuse for any further delay.

A tall range man with pale, almost golden stubble fringing his square jaw, had watched everything from a little way down the bar. Now he motioned to the barkeep. When Burl came down, the stubbled man said,

'What the hell you pamperin' this son of a bitch for? Look what he done to Casey.'

'You just answered your own question, Montana.'

Montana straightened. He had a longish face and big teeth, giving a slight impression of a horse. Some had

9

even likened his rare laughter to a neigh — but they whispered that. 'You bein' smart with me?'

Burl lifted a placating hand quickly. 'No, no. But he could be just what we been lookin' for. No one else ever laid out that bastard Casey.'

Montana glanced at Cade again, frowning, then nodded slowly. 'Could be, could be. Gimme another shot and a chaser before you go.'

Cade was swaying a little now, holding on to the edge of the bar, eyes looking slightly out of focus.

But he rinsed with two more slugs of the 'special' hooch the barkeep served, and then four men guided him outside, half-dragging him to the narrow stairs leading to the dentist's rooms.

Payne lived up to his name — in looks, anyway. His face seemed contorted in a permanent grimace and his mouth moved in what might have been the beginning of a smile. It briefly disappeared when they told him how Cade had gunwhipped Bull Casey to

10

the floor and then his lips peeled back to reveal yellow teeth.

'You shall be my special patient, friend. Put him in the chair, gents.' He worked a lever and Cade yelled as the back collapsed and he stretched out on the leather with a jar that brought a groan and a curse from him.

'It's all right, friend. Try to relax. I know my job.' Payne gestured at the men to hold Cade's arms while he fumbled at a tall metal cylinder with a thin rubber tube attached. He fitted it to a padded leather face mask and clamped it across Cade's nose as the cowboy felt the waves of rising panic begin to swamp even the drum-beating agony of his molar. He bucked and struggled, made gurgling noises but gradually subsided as the gas began to take effect.

'I think maybe a double dose of our laughing gas is in order,' Doc Payne announced. He opened the tank spigot a little more and the hissing sound increased.

'I don't think he's gonna be laffin', Doc,' one of the townsmen said as Cade began to kick and struggle again. Then, suddenly, he went limp and his muffled curses faded to a kind of sighing moan . . .

'Hand me those forceps, will you, Jed . . . ?'

Jed picked up the instrument indicated and looked sharply at the dentist. 'Forceps! These here are reg'lar ol' fencin' pliers!'

Payne smiled a little sheepishly as he took them and began to push them into Cade's now slack mouth. 'They do the job — so what matter? *He* won't know the difference.' As he clamped the jaws on the crumbling tooth, a deep moan began in Cade's chest and quickly rose to a strangled roar. Jed jumped back a pace.

'Why anyone'd call it *laffin'* gas beats the hell outta me!'

Some of this drifted through Cade's half-anaesthetized brain but was quickly lost as the gas took hold. Whirling, bright colours dazzled him. A train whistle, shrieked. Flashes of strange incidents from his life flickered behind his eyes, and other, dream-like apparitions caused him to moan and squirm in the semi-delirium induced by the massive dose of nitrous oxide . . .

There were many wild glimpses of scenes from his childhood, glimmers of more nightmarish creatures, all mixed up in a swirl of fear, and he giggled and moaned stupidly.

Half-remembered war scenes made him tense and writhe as the dentist worked over him. Then he felt as if he was choking; the memory of a madly-tossing steer's horn gouging his ribs brought a loud cry of pain from his bloody mouth. He fell into some dark, dank place: clung desperately to a box-car door on a rocking train as it careered down a mountain, followed by a heart-stopping drop off a redbluff cliff into swirling, muddy waters. *Which river? Rio? Red? Brazos . . . .?* Take your pick: they'd all tried to kill him at one time or another. Then everything was black — black — black . . . a kind of limbo. Nothing — only a strange feeling of suspension and no place to go . . .

These were no more than impressions that jammed up his throbbing brain until he saw a dim glow that drew his attention, dragged his consciousness back from wherever that son of a bitch of a dentist had sent him with his foul gas . . .

He only retained vague memories of his experience, felt wrung-out, battered, sick, confused by all the chopsuey imagery after he eventually came round. He was fully clothed, sitting up in a narrow bed, the sheets all rumpled.

There was a burning oil lamp somewhere close with the wick turned too high, tendrils of black sooty smoke drifting around his throbbing face, tingling his nostrils.

He looked down, hazily saw there was a wooden tray across his thighs with some papers on it. He was holding a pen and a hairy-fingered hand held out a small stone inkwell towards him. 'Dip 'er in, *amigo*.'

It even hurt to raise his eyes. 'Where'm I . . . ?'

'In the recovery room behind the dentist's,' a strange voice said. Through a haze, he saw there were two other men dressed in frock coats and vests standing by his bed. It was the closest one who had spoken. 'Just sign at the bottom of the page, Mr Cade — Burl will help you — and then you can sleep for as long as you like.'

A firm grip guided his unresisting hand towards the top paper on the tray. 'That's it, *amigo*. Sign your name.'

Head spinning as the pen began to move instinctively in a scrawl, an insistent juddering pain beating behind his eyes, Chris Cade felt the third man fumbling at his shirt front.

'Wha'a' hell?' he slurred, tongue all swollen and still half-numbed in his bloody mouth. Something pricked his left breast. 'Heeey! Tha' hurt!'

Squinting down, he saw that the third

man had pinned a metal star to his shirt pocket. Now the man stepped back.

'Congratulations, Mr Cade. You are now Sheriff of Reno Creek.'

2

Room With a View

It was full daylight when Cade opened his eyes again. Those extra hours of sleep had cleared his head some, but he still felt muzzy, like after a two-day bender at the end of a long, hard trail drive.

The dentist reminded him he was now a sheriff. 'We offered you the job and you accepted without hesitation.'

'Don' 'member.' Cade rubbed his forehead, tongue inside his mouth exploring the mangled space where his molar used to be. 'Ouch! Sumpin prick my tongue.'

'That'll be catgut, Sheriff,' Dentist Payne told him. 'Had to cut your gum to get the abscess drained. I'll pull the stitches in a day or two.'

Cade lifted stony eyes towards the

man. 'Mebbe.' He looked just as bleakly at the other two men in the room. 'Why're you railroadin' me into this lawman's job?'

This man now held the paper he vaguely recalled trying to sign with help from Burl. Payne had told him the distinguished-looking man was Judge Ethan Kirk, chairman of the town council, adding, 'Burl here, our biggest saloon owner, and myself are also members. There's a couple others, too.'

There were grey streaks in Kirk's hair; he had a paunch straining against his flowered vest and a good quality coat hanging loose. He smelled of rich cigars and whiskey.

'Our former sheriff was — er — accidentally killed recently, and we've been looking for a replacement.'

Cade frowned, the small muscle movement hurting his swollen face. 'You dunno nothin' 'bout me.'

They grinned: his words were only slightly slurred now though he felt his tongue had to work to get them out so they could be readily understood.

'I think we know enough, Chris Cade. Born Flagstaff, Arizona, thirty-some years ago; went on the drift early, following the cattle trails; made quite a name for yourself as a top cowhand. Did a spell in both the army and the Texas Rangers, during which time you killed the notorious outlaw and murderer, Blaze McKinley, in a gunfight . . . '

The judge paused as Cade lifted one hand. 'Not just me. Took four of us to nail McKinley.'

The councillors exchanged glances, perhaps mildly perturbed at their mistake, but Burl, the saloon man said,

'You mentioned your Captain of Troop — Hedley Morriso. Man, now there is a name known the length and breadth of the U-nited States. You had to be good to be in his troop.'

Cade frowned, one hand lightly holding his swollen face. The flesh felt hot. 'I told you all this?'

'Sure, when you were under the gas.

19

Happens all the time,' Payne assured him. He winked. 'Some of the secrets I've learned from local patients! If I had a notion to blackmail, reckon I'd be retired an' livin' it up by now.'

That brought a chuckle from the others, but not from Cade.

'What else'd I say?' Cade sounded wary, maybe even worried. *Afraid he'd let something slip he didn't mean to while under the influence of the dental gas . . . ?*

'Aw, few things. Little hard to figure out for sure — your words were all slurred — but you listened OK when we put it to you to take the sheriff's job.' Burl looked at his companions. 'Sounded downright eager, din' he, gents?'

'Surely did,' agreed the judge.

'Dead keen,' added Doc Payne.

Cade was silent, frowning, looking pale and obviously still in a good deal of pain and not yet quite fully clear in his mind from the after-effects of the gas.

'What's the job pay?'

Burl and Payne looked to the judge who cleared his throat. 'Fifty a month.' When Cade's frown deepened and the man gave him that frigid stare again, Judge Kirk added quickly, 'Includes a room with, er, full service, in Burl's saloon. Or, if that doesn't appeal, there's a cabin you can have the use of. We'd have to fix it up some first, but — '

'Had a pard was marshal of Wichita once. They paid him a hundred a month, all found, even to supplying his ammunition.'

'Ah, yes! But — Wichita! Well, I mean, that's a hell town. Reno Creek can't be compared to that. But maybe fifty is a little low . . . ' The judge arched his eyebrows at Burl and Payne and they nodded briefly. 'S'pose we make it sixty?'

'Eighty and all found.'

The judge clamped his blubbery lips. 'That gas seems to have worn off mighty fast, Doc!' he snapped accusingly.

Payne cleared his throat. 'Does that sometimes. But, listen, Cade, we're trying to do you a favour and here you are holdin' us up — '

'*Who* you doing the favour . . . ?'

'Well — we'll all benefit, naturally, the town in particular,' said Burl Randall. 'Look, settle for sixty-five and I think we might have a deal. OK with you gents?'

Judge Kirk and Payne nodded reluctantly and all eyes turned to Cade.

He let them sweat a little before agreeing with a grunt. He squinted at the paper — the contract, presumably — and held out his hand towards the judge.

'Better make the change here.' He took the paper before the judge could get a tight grip and squinted at the bottom. 'This hen-scratchin' s'posed to be my name?'

'You wrote it,' said Ethan Kirk, then suddenly smiled, perking up. 'Why, now, just a minute, you've signed that contract and the rate mentioned is fifty dollars a month . . . So it's legally binding, and we could hold you to that.'

While the judge was smirking, Cade looked at the scribble on the bottom of the paper. The ink bottle with the pen handle protruding from it was still on the small table beside the bed. He stretched across, took the pen, wet with fresh ink, and vigorously scratched out his signature, blotting it completely.

'Not a legal document now, Judge. Signature can't be read, so the paper means nothing. Only good to hang in the privy.'

'Now you hold up a goddamn minute!' Kirk's fat jowls shook as his face darkened with anger, tight with rising fury. 'What're you trying to pull, Cade?'

All three exchanged worried glances and despite his pain and the fresh stab of agony from moving his mouth into a crooked smile, Cade slowly crumpled the paper.

'Best write a fresh agreement, gents. Seventy, I believe we settled on . . . '

'Now, listen, feller . . . '

'Ah, write a new one, Judge,' growled Burl. 'He *did* gunwhip Bull Casey and that's gotta count for somethin'.'

'Burl's right, Judge,' said Payne. 'We can . . . afford it.'

'I'm not going to stand still for a shakedown like this!' Judge Ethan Kirk glared at his fellow councillors, jerked his head and they moved just out of Cade's hearing. 'I'm not so sure he's going to be as 'suitable' as we first thought.'

Burl smiled faintly and said in a whisper, 'Well, Casey ain't gonna forget that gunwhippin' in a hurry, Judge. He'll be keen to square things — if the need arose, I mean — and the deal was to his likin' . . . '

Doc Payne and the judge nodded gently.

'As long as we've got something we can fall back on,' Kirk allowed quietly. 'But I'm not letting him off with this.' He raised his voice, 'All right, Cade, I'll write a new contract, *but it will be sixty-five dollars a month*. Take it or leave it.'

Burl and Doc Payne looked a little

startled at Kirk laying it on the line like this. They watched Chris Cade's lop-sided face as he stared back at them, finally nodding.

'OK. It's better'n stayin' broke, I guess.' He studied the trio as they bent over the judge's shoulder while he wrote out the new contract. He closed his eyes as if the dregs of the gas in his system had hit him with a wave of sleepiness. He cocked his ears but heard nothing to his advantage.

Well, he'd done all kinds of jobs over the past twenty years, cajoled and negotiated payment for many different deals — but this was the first time he had been a cut-price lawman . . .

Maybe if he was smart — and careful — he could make a quick stake and then move on . . .

There was little he liked about Reno Creek so far, and he had an uncomfort-able idea that it wasn't going to get any better.

★　★　★

He stalled them for three days, pretending only half the time that the sudden bouts of 'sleepiness' from residual gas in his system were genuine: the rest of the time they were genuine. But the councillors were smart enough to leave him to 'sleep it off' and discussed nothing within his hearing that might tell him just what they really had in mind for him . . .

Brain only partly functioning, he already had figured that whatever it was, he was going to have to *earn* the money they had agreed to pay him, however much or little.

But he'd stick for a spell, get a few bucks together, then, when it suited him, he'd move on. That contract didn't mean a thing, not the way they had coerced him into signing.

But that was OK: two could play at that game.

And he was not without experience . . .

When he finally left the stuffy, cupboard-like room behind Payne's, he wasn't as unsteady on his feet as he made out.

Burl Randall had sent a man to bring his gear up to the room in the back of the saloon that Cade had opted for, rather than the barely-liveable cabin on the outskirts of town. The man must be one of the saloon's bouncers, Cade decided, looking at the battered face with the scars of old wounds around the eyes, the nose with a lean to starboard and the gaps between the man's teeth. No, he was wrong: no saloon lackey wore a six-gun in that kind of fast draw rig. And he did look vaguely familiar: said his name was 'Crowe'.

'Spelt with an 'e'. I ain't got no Injun blood in me.'

Which told him something about Crowe, but he didn't figure it was worth remembering. The room was on the first floor, back, and could be reached by either the normal stairway from the barroom, or by a rickety set of stairs fixed to the clapboard rear wall, then through a narrow door.

It looked comfortable enough and had a small window.

Crowe seemed to be hanging around and Cade gave him a level look: 'If you want a tip, come back later. I don't have a plugged nickel right now.'

'Keep your damn tip. I was just thinkin' I seen you somewheres before.'
And I've seen you, too, Cade thought.

'Might be — I've been around. Passed through here with a couple trailherds under 'Boss' Fredericks.'

The man nodded slightly. 'I'll recollect. You want your grub sent up? Or you gonna eat downstairs? I ain't no message boy but the judge told me to ask.'

So, Crowe was the judge's man . . . .
'I'll eat up here.'

Crowe grunted and went out. Cade started to unpack his warbag, hanging his spare clothing on nails driven into the wall behind a drab curtain strung across a corner.

Nothing seemed to be missing, not even the old, stained Army jacket he had stuffed into one saddle-bag. He hung it on a nail over his slicker, then went downstairs and asked Burl to send up a hip bath and lots of hot water.

A fat Indian squaw brought the tin tub first, carrying it without effort, although Cade instinctively went to help her. Her dark eyes flashed and then softened a little at his offered courtesy. She shook her head, set it in the middle of the floor and went out. She returned with two buckets of steaming water, left, came back with a bucket of cold water and set it down beside the bath after handing him a curved bar of kerosene soap and a thin towel.

When the door had closed behind her, he stripped off his trail clothes and lowered himself into the hot water, sucking a sharp breath that sent a shaft of cool air through the hole left by his old molar. He had been on a soup and mush diet and was getting tired of it, hoped Crowe would have the sense to tell the cook to send up a decent meal.

He leaned back against the sloping tub, closed his eyes and soon dozed.

He didn't know how much later he heard the peremptory knock on the door before it opened. Blinking, half awake, he saw a woman entering with a tray of food. It smelled savoury and he sat up, making sure his nether regions were decorously masked by the soapy water. On the tray was some kind of fish, mashed potatoes and peas.

He sucked down a sharp breath: she must be one of the bar girls, he figured, the low-cut bodice of her frilly red-and-green dress revealing a good deal of milky-white flesh, and the beginning of cleavage. She smiled, lips red with paint, but only a touch of rouge on her high cheekbones, maybe a little powder on the rest of her face.

'Howdy, Sheriff. Brought your supper.'

'Fine.' He cleared his throat hurriedly. 'Just set it down on the bedside table.'

She did so and turned to look down

at him. 'Need your back scrubbed?' Her smile widened and she shook her head, black hair briefly falling across one side of her face. 'I come with the room, if you want any . . . extras. Call me 'Wiley'.'

'What kinda name's that for a nice-lookin' gal?'

'Oh, you noticed I'm a gal, huh? Wondered. You seen one of these lately?' He sat up straighter in the tub as she pulled down one side of her bodice, revealing a nicely rounded, pale breast with a pink tip.

He swallowed. 'Usually come in pairs, if I recollect right.' His voice had a hoarse rasp to it now.

'You've got a good memory.'

He simply stared as she pushed the bodice down almost to her waist. His breath hissed through his nostrils. Because of that damn tooth: it had ached for weeks and it had been a long time since he had seen a woman like this . . .

Well, if they were being so consider-ate of his needs this way, he figured he really was going to have to work hard for his money. They must have more plans than simply having him wear a badge around Reno Creek ... But what ... ?

She was now struggling out of her dress and underwear. 'Reckon there'll be enough room in there for me?'

He smiled crookedly, not even noticing the twitch of pain in his jaw.

'If you kinda kneel down, right in front of me. Might slop the water some, though.'

Her smile widened as she stepped into the tub. 'You can bet on that!'

3

Whose Law?

Chris Cade took a walk around the streets after breakfast, the badge prominently on display against the blue of the new denim shirt he had bought last night at Latham's General Store.

As he'd waited for the counterman to wrap his shirt, along with a pair of corduroy trousers, he took down a hat and, while he fitted it and curled the brim to his liking, glanced at the price tags on the various goods.

'Prices seem a mite high,' he commented and the assistant, young, still with acne scars showing on his oval face amidst some soft early stubble, looked up blankly. When the sheriff adjusted the hat one final time, and he said no more, the shop assistant licked his lips.

'We are a trail town, as you already know, Sheriff. It's accepted that prices rise when a trail herd hits any town.'

'No herd here, so these are everyday prices, ain't they?' The shop assistant nodded, looking wary now. 'Just about every item here can be had cheaper down trail at Sunset. Difference'd even make it worth the ride.'

'Er, you want I should get Mr Latham?'

Cade shook his head. 'Mebbe later. How much?'

He had had an advance against his pay and brought out some bills and coins. The counterman, hesitated, then, grasping a page torn from his receipt book, turned and hurried out back. 'Be with you in a minute, Sheriff.'

Cade waited: he knew what was coming, debated briefly how he would react, decided to go along. He figured it would be expected of him and this was as good a chance as any to find out if the word had been passed along to 'take care' of the new sheriff.

The kid came back smiling. 'An even five dollars, Sheriff.'

'You had schoolin' in addin' up?'

The kid blinked, looked blank, then grinned, lowering his voice. 'Actually comes to seven or eight bucks, but Mr Latham said seein' as you're the new law around here, he'll give you a cut in price. He's throwin' in the hat for free.'

Cade nodded, placed the money on the counter, pocketed the rest and picked up his parcel. 'Tell Latham I'm obliged. Helps make up for some of the times he's robbed me when I've come through with a trail herd.'

He saw a shadowy movement at the end of the aisle where the entry to the storeroom was and tossed off a two-fingered salute from the brim of his new hat. The shadow disappeared and he wondered why Latham didn't come and introduce himself.

Still on trial . . . he figured silently as he went out into the street.

Now, dressed in his new clothes and with the hat cocked a little over his left eye he strolled along, familiarizing himself with the town again. He nodded to folk, passing a few words here and there: most seemed a mite leery of him. A couple acknowledged him with no more than a curt nod; most of the women looked away, yet still checked him out.

His face was still swollen and bruised from Doc Payne's tender ministrations, but the smoke from his now burning cigarette seemed to soothe the residual pain in the molar socket. He had stubble and his hair was hanging over his collar: maybe not the best image of a new lawman.

He paused on the edge of the boardwalk at an intersection, leaned a shoulder against an awning post and looked around.

He could see two saloons, one of them Burl Randall's The Buckjumpin' Gal, showed a faded painting depicting a scantily-clad girl rough-rider in the saddle of a wildly bucking bronco. He smiled faintly, wondering how the town's matrons liked that revealing painting. Looking closer, he thought maybe Wiley could have been the model for the artist . . . *He figured the name suited her, too.*

The second saloon was smaller than Burl's, needed some paint and had a few boards nailed over the front window, which showed some broken edges. It was called, simply, Fancy's. It didn't seem to be open for custom yet, although the Buckjumpin' Gal was doing good business.

He went up one side of Main and back down the other, looking in the windows of the stores, spending a little time studying the weapons displayed in the gun-smith's streetfront window. He found a barber's, decided to have a hair trim and a shave, went in and sat down on a form where three other shaggy customers waited. The barber offered to take him first but Cade shook his head. 'No hurry.'

The barber looked slightly non-plussed, then one of the other men stood and sat in the chair, glaring. He had light golden stubble and long sandy hair. Cade tried to recall where he'd seen him before recently. He looked tough — and touchy. 'You ever learn how to count, Baldy?'

'Just offering the new sheriff a little consideration, Montana.'

'Show it to your reg'lar customers, then,' Montana grunted, looking straight at Cade. The barber, now red-faced, worked up a lather in the shaving cup, looking a mite worried. Eventually it was Cade's turn and, strangely for a man in his trade, the barber had little to say, sticking to the weather and the condition of the trail. When he had finished, Cade paid the price showing on the wall board and went looking for the law office.

He found it halfway along Main, squeezed between a drapery and a saddler's. No wonder he had missed it earlier: there was only a small twelve-by-five inch hand-painted sign that said *Sheriff* nailed beside the door.

Inside it smelled musty and there was

a thin layer of dust on the desk and its papers, the two chairs and a gun cabinet, the door of which was locked.

He found a rag and dusted off the swivel chair behind the desk. A shadow darkened the doorway and he looked up quickly, squinting, and saw it was the man the barber had called Montana.

'You following me?'

'I got no interest in you, lawman.'

'Then you might's well go.'

Montana stiffened. 'Listen, you! Don't figure you can throw your weight around just because you got that tin star pinned on your shirt.'

'It's my shirt. What d'you want, Montana?'

'Courtesy call.'

'I'm all outta courtesy. Busy settling in. You from one of the ranches?'

Montana's pale green eyes were slitted now. He didn't answer at first, then nodded curtly. 'Ramrod for the Padlock. Pat Magruder's spread.'

The name meant nothing to Cade right then.

Montana suddenly whirled and strode away. Cade went to the door, watched him stomp back towards the saloon, then sat down at his desk and started to go through some of the papers strewn across it. They listed expected times of arriving trail herds; stageline schedules with the strongbox-carrying dates ringed in indelible pencil; Saturdays on a ragged calendar were marked with various ranch names: J Bar, Pothook, Cross 9, Padlock — probably when their crews would be in town after payday. Someone had had enough sense to stagger them so that all the range crews didn't hit the streets of Reno Creek on the same day.

Then once again a shadow fell across the desk and he snapped his head up, right hand dropping towards his gun-butt. A man he'd never seen before stood silhouetted against the sunlit street.

'So you're the one they got to replace him.'

He was a medium-sized man, coming slowly but determinedly into the office, dressed like a town businessman: checked vest over a white shirt with sleevebands keeping the cuffs from hanging too low over his bony wrists. He looked about forty, had thinning hair combed across to cover his bald patch. His face was narrow, pinched with worry, the eyes steady and cool.

'I'm Sheriff Cade, the new law here. Who're you?'

The man snorted. 'Which 'law' would that be? The one in the official book? Or mebbe just the kind the town council wants?'

'I — am — the — law,' Cade said firmly. 'I'll have to study the book some and the town ordinance, if there is one, but that's the kind of law I'll be pushin'.'

The man frowned, then shook his head slowly. 'Sounds good anyway.'

'Which means?'

'Well, if the council appointed you, without an election, you're their man! You'll do what they say, no matter what's printed in any book.'

Cade held the belligerent stare, let the silence drag some, then when he figured the man was ready to speak again, cut in curtly, 'I asked who you are.'

'The name Hawkins mean anything to you?' When Cade shook his head slowly, the man almost spat his next words: 'It's *my* name! Shelby Hawkins. My brother Mel was the sheriff here, till he . . . died.'

Cade nodded. 'Some kinda accident wasn't it?'

Shelby Hawkins frowned, seemed to go very still.

' 'Some kinda accident . . . ?' They didn't even tell you about it . . . ?'

Cade shook his head. Hawkins's face was pale and tight now, his hands clenched down at his sides. 'The sons of bitches! My brother was duly elected, the folk here wanted him in office! But that didn't suit Judge Kirk an' his damn 'council'! My brother was *honest*! Straight from the shoulder, a fair man, made sure any woman could walk around this town, day or night, and not have to worry about drunks or hard-cases botherin' her.'

'Must've been a busy man.'

'Damn right! An' they used it against him in the end.' He paused expectantly but Cade waited in silence for an explanation. Hawkins's voice had a small tremor in it when he continued: 'Some of the ranches figured a horse race through town to celebrate the tenth year of the town's settlement'd be a good idea. Mel said OK, laid out strict rules and which streets would be used, even arranged for a big bullock-roast picnic to follow.'

'Sounds good.'

'Yes! But they fixed it so my brother should start the race and they also fixed it for a half-wild stallion from McGruder's Padlock spread to break loose from the line and stomp Mel into the goddamn ground!'

Cade straightened in the chair, seeing the grief-sparked anger making Hawkins's entire rawboned frame shake. The man could hardly speak, breath coming in ragged gasps.

'That sounds like it could be a genuine accident. A half-broke hoss shouldn't've been allowed in the race. I guess all the noise and so on could've scared it — '

'That's what happened! An' to make sure it was good an' scared, someone threw a firecracker under its belly. No one ever found out who but it set that stallion off like he'd had a red hot iron shoved up his ass!'

'Better calm down, Shelby,' Cade told him coolly.

The man stepped forward, leaned his hands on the edge of the desk, glaring at the new lawman.

'It — was — no — accident! It was meant to happen just the way it did.'

'Something like that would be mighty hard to arrange in front of the whole damn town. I guess everyone was there?'

Hawkins nodded, breath hissing through flared nostrils as he tried to keep some measure of calm. 'Yeah, everyone saw it! Everyone said, 'Poor Sheriff Hawkins, in the wrong place at the wrong time!' Hell almighty! 'Course he was! But it was *arranged*, I tell you!'

Cade watched the man closely, not sure which way Hawkins was going to jump. 'You'd have a hard job proving it, I reckon.'

Shelby Hawkins reared back, turned completely around, driven by his frustrated anger. 'That's somethin' we agree on! But I'll do it. I'll find out why they wanted him dead — apart from putting in a new sheriff that they can control.'

There was a challenge there and Cade forced himself not to rise to the prodding.

'I'm my own man, Hawkins,' he said evenly. 'Anyone who says different is either a liar — or a damn fool.'

He stood slowly and Hawkins had to look up to see his hard-set face, lopsided still with the swelling of his jaw. Shelby Hawkins moved back a pace, lip curling.

'Sure! And if I was stupid enough to reach for my gun you'd shoot me down and I'd be outta Judge Kirk's hair for good. Fortuntately, I don't wear a gun.'

'Mebbe you'd beat me to the draw.'

Hawkins laughed harshly. 'Oh, yeah? Hell, I'm no gunfighter! No damn fool, neither, so I won't push it. You hear? I won't push it!'

'Then take some advice, mister. Keep your mouth shut, or bring me proof of what you say.'

Hawkins stared and then shook his head in open disbelief. 'That'd really be my death warrant, wouldn't it? Aaah! You can go to hell!' He turned and started for the door, then swung back. 'I'll get the proof, eventually, and when I do, it won't be you I bring it to. I'll call in the US marshal from Kinlaw, the county seat!'

He slammed the door behind him and Cade sat down again, frowning.

'Well, that's a good start to the day,' he said aloud.

He found dog-eared copies of the town ordinance and a *Handbook of State Law* in the back of a cupboard. He figured by the amount of dust and the way the spines had been eaten by cockroaches that it had been a long, long time since anyone studied these.

He made notes as he worked his way through the ordinance and was checking them when Crowe lurched in.

'Judge wants to see you.'

'I'll be through here shortly.'

'He said 'now'.'

Cade shot a steelly stare at the ugly messenger. 'I'll be along shortly.'

Crowe dropped a hand towards his gunbutt, then froze as he stared into the muzzle of Cade's cocked six-shooter, rock steady in the lawman's right hand. He frowned, swallowed and let breath hiss through his teeth as he held both hands well out from his sides.

'Well, well. Judge has hired himself a real gun-fighter an' I bet he don't realize it.' He lifted two fingers towards his scarred forehead and jerked them in

47

a brief salute. 'OK, feller, I'll give him your message.'

Cade holstered his Colt as Crowe went out. He continued making notes, dusted off the *Handbook of State Law* and flicked through the pages briefly. He gathered up the lot and folded the papers into a shirt pocket, took down his hat and set it on his head of thick brown hair, still smelling of the barber's bay rum.

Judge Kirk was waiting for him at the council chambers, a set of rooms at the back of the community hall on Brazos Street which ran parallel to Main. Kirk did not seem in a happy mood. He glanced at his gold pocket watch, then glared at Cade. Crowe was seated on a chair in a corner, an amused look barely discernible on his battered face.

'Twenty minutes since I sent word I wanted to see you!' the judge snapped.

Cade sat down in a straightback chair and pushed his hat to the back of his head. 'Was familiarizing myself with your ordinance and a few points of law, Judge.'

Kirk frowned. 'You leave that sort of thing to me and the council. We'll tell you what needs doing.'

Cade shook his head briefly. 'Reckon you'll tell me what you *want* doing, which ain't necessarily what *needs* doin'.'

Kirk interlocked his fingers, forearms on his big cedar desk. His shoulders hunched as he leaned towards the sheriff. 'Who've you been talking to?'

'Hawkins was in his office earlier,' Crowe offered.

The judge's shoulders tensed even more. 'Cade, I could've made a mistake about you. I don't make many mistakes, but when I do, I set 'em right, fast as I can. You understand?'

Cade savvied, all right: the judge was angry, but it was petty anger, edged with rising panic. He and his cronies had figured they were hiring themselves a puppet because of the condition he was in when he arrived: bedevilled by the rotten tooth and the belly-rotting booze, both enhanced by that damn gas. He must have appeared to be an easy mark.

Now, Kirk was wondering just what kind of a pig-in-a-poke he'd bought himself.

'I'm trying to do the job you hired me for, Judge.' Cade took his notes from his shirt pocket and unfolded the papers. 'Been checking the town ordinance so's I'll know what's what . . . '

Judge Kirk nodded a mite jerkily, but forced himself to say, 'Well, I find that commendable, but when I send — '

'And I don't think it's legal,' Cade cut in, his words making Kirk's eyes bulge.

'Legal? I drew up those rules myself with the help of the finest lawyer in this part of the country!'

Cade looked dubious. 'This here for a start, Judge: 'No one will carry a firearm of any description within the town limits when a trail herd is in town, or at such other times as determined by local law.' Sounds reasonable enough at first. Then when I looked up the penalties for breaching it: 'Five dollar fine for first offence; a week's gaol and twenty dollars for the second. Third — if anyone's stupid enough to push it that far — a sentence to be decided by the court, which shall be served in the State Penitentiary and/or on the current chain gang . . . ' 'Cade looked up and met Kirk's stony stare. 'Kinda rough, Judge. Big fines and slave labour.'

'I mean to keep this town law-abiding — *my* way! And I have the full backing of the council, which, incidentally, overrides the local lawman.'

Cade nodded slowly. 'And the fines? What happens to that money?'

Kirk's face reddened. 'By God, who the hell do you think you're talking to! You are the sheriff! As such you keep the peace on the streets, do what you're told and collect your pay on the first of each month. That seems simple enough, surely.'

Cade scratched lightly at the still

swollen side of his face. 'Guess so, but I figure my job is to enforce the town ordinance — '

'Correct! Under orders decided by the town council.'

Cade smiled thinly. 'Can't find anythin' in state law that says that, Judge.'

Kirk's shoulders hunched again as he looked like he was going to climb over his desk to get at Cade. 'The mistake you've made, *Sheriff* Cade, is that you haven't realized *I* am the law here! You are no more than a tool I use to enforce it. And you do so, sir, as *directed*!'

Chris Cade flipped through his pages, knowing the judge was steaming at this deliberate delay.

'Do you understand yet?'

Cade stood slowly, 'Beginnin' to, Judge.'

'Sit down! I haven't finished with you. You've overstepped the mark by criticizing Ed Latham's prices.' He paused but the sheriff said nothing. 'Man, he was even decent enough to give you a discount, to make you feel welcome! He is one of our most respected businessmen, a member of my council, and he feels, as I do, that there's an apology due.'

'Sorry he feels that way, Judge,' Cade said turning towards the door. With his hand on the knob, he glanced back. 'You, too. There are trail herds due soon. A lot of men I used to work with'll be ridin' with 'em. I've been gypped by this town many times when I was working trail up this way. Now I'm in a position to see that trail riders get a square deal. Reckon the folk who live here will appreciate a drop in prices to a more reasonable level, too.'

'People who live in trail towns expect high prices.' The judge's hard eyes locked with Cade's. 'Everyone benefits in the long run.'

He let that hang, looking steadily at Cade, who chose to ignore the implication that 'everyone' included him.

He smiled crookedly and left without comment. Crowe sat there, looking at the seething judge. 'I *know* I've seen that ranny someplace, Judge . . . I'll remember eventually.'

'Casey out of the infirmary yet?'

'Yeah, an' he'll snap your head off an' use it as a doorstop, you even mention Cade's name.'

'Get him.'

4

Challenge

Cade took a chance and ordered stew for his supper, pleasantly surprised to find that, not only could he chew it without it hurting his still tender jaw, but it was genuinely tasty. He had a slice of deep-dish apple pie for dessert and smoked a cigar he had bought earlier on the narrow balcony outside his room.

He hadn't seen Wiley but figured he wouldn't go looking. Her job in the saloon would take priority anyway, although Burl Randall had stopped by in the late afternoon to ask if everything was satisfactory.

'Feel like I'm gettin' the royal treatment, Burl.'

Randall glanced at him carefully for a moment and then shrugged. 'Why not?

You're gonna take care of the town, so it's only fair we take care of you. Let me know if there's anythin' you need.'

Cade nodded and pursed his lips as the man went back down to his bar, wondering if Burl had talked with the judge since he had left the council rooms . . .

The saloon man seemed genuinely solicitous but it could be all part of the plan to make him feel 'welcome', get him 'on side' as it were.

After he had finished the cigar he oiled and cleaned his Colt, then took a walk through the town. There were quite a few folk strolling in the balmy evening. He touched his hat brim to several ladies, a couple of whom elbowed their husbands or escorts in the ribs, as if to say, 'Why aren't you as courteous as our new sheriff?'

Mostly the men seemed wary of him, a few indifferent and a couple openly hostile.

Then he went into the bar of Burl's saloon, figuring to have a drink or two before going back to his room.

Randall himself was behind the counter and reached under and brought up a bottle of reddish liquor. Cade held up a hand quickly.

'Tooth's all taken care of, Burl.'

Randall chuckled. 'This ain't that drain cleaner I gave you before. This is good hooch, genuine Kentucky bourbon. Thought you might like it with a beer chaser.'

'Think I might agree with you.' Cade reached automatically into his pocket but even as Burl poured him an overflowing shotglass, the saloon man said,

'On the house — and whatever else you want.'

Cade looked steadily at him, placed a half-dollar on the counter. 'Thanks all the same, Burl, but I'll pay.'

Randall frowned and several drinkers close by paused, waiting to see what happened next.

'Heard the judge give you a rough time.'

'Thought he figured that's what I gave him.'

Burl smiled crookedly. 'Just got off on the wrong foot. I'm tryin' to set it straight.'

'Then take my money.'

Randall was sober now. 'Listen, Chris, mebbe things aren't just as we might've figured, but I'm just tryin' to smoothe 'em over. You play along and you'll find it's the best deal you've come across in a — ' He stopped abruptly, looking past Cade's shoulder. 'Dammit, Casey! I thought I told you you was barred from my saloon!'

Cade turned quickly.

Big Bull Casey was walking towards his position at the bar, a wave of silence washing after him, conversation dying abruptly. Casey's face had some strips of plaster covering the gashes that had needed stitching. Both eyes had dark bruises underneath; his nose was still swollen and looked mighty tender. His lips were puffy around scabbing sores.

Now Casey stopped as Cade faced

him. He ignored Burl Randall and lifted his left arm pointing a thick finger at the sheriff. 'I got somethin' to square with you, mister.'

'Forget it,' advised Cade quietly. 'That way we'll both save ourselves a lot of trouble.'

Casey snorted. 'I got a *problem* with you, but you're the one gonna have the trouble.'

Casey's right hand hovered over his Colt butt as he waved his left hand in an attempt to distract the sheriff. It didn't work and Burl started to bring up his sawn-off shotgun from under the counter.

'Leave it, Burl!' Cade snapped without turning his head.

'Dammit, Chris, he shouldn't even be in here!'

Cade nodded at Casey. 'You gonna draw?'

The big man frowned: he hadn't expected this. He figured he would draw and shoot while Cade was distracted by his waving left hand, but now, with Cade ready, *No sir!*

'Reckon not!' Casey said in sudden decision and he lunged forward, taking everyone by surprise, moving a lot faster than Cade would have thought possible. 'For now!'

The bully's solid body slammed into Cade and drove him back against the bar. The zinc edge cut into his back, making his spine creak, and for an instant he felt a wave of nausea surge through him.

Then the pain was transferred to his face as Casey's big right fist came across his body and exploded against the swelling on his already traumatized jaw. The pain was intense and his ears rang; his brain seemed suddenly loose in his skull and his legs buckled. Casey bulled in, chopping a blow down at Cade's head. The new hat went flying and the clubbed hand battered his skull. The sawdusted floor leapt up to meet him. He had enough instinct to half turn and take the impact mostly on one shoulder, but his head still rapped the brass footrail and a whole new comet-trail of colours seared behind his eyes.

Someone yelled a warning and, through a red haze, Cade glimpsed the heavy boot driving at his face. He threw himself in a twisting movement and the boot scraped across his upper left arm and part of his back before jarring against the footrail. It threw Casey off balance and he clawed at the bar edge. Burl Randall contrived to slam the heavy base of a beer glass across those splayed, sausage-thick fingers. Casey howled, and snatched the hand against his chest while still trying to remain steady on his feet.

Suddenly Cade came up, close in, rising fast, and his skull caught Casey's lantern jaw. The impact of clashing teeth was heard clearly, as his head snapped back. The big man staggered as Cade's fist took him in the chest, and another gave his nose a decided slant to starboard.

Still a little groggy, Cade closed in,

legs spread, fists hammering at the stitched face, his knuckles ripping loose the plaster strips. Flesh burned and stitches tore loose. Blood flowed and Casey lurched away, with a roar, hands clawing in an attempt to cover up. Cade went after him relentlessly, arms working in a blur as he hammered blow after blow into the man's big body.

Crowe, on the edge of the yelling crowd, narrowed his eyes and craned his thick neck for a better view.

'Why the hell din' he keep punchin' Casey's ugly face?' yelled the man next to Crowe, as Cade switched to blurring body blows. It was Montana from the barber's shop.

Crowe glared. 'Got more sense than to break his hands on a bonehead like Casey. He'll punch his lungs out first, then finish him with an uppercut.'

'Yeah?' Montana seemed sceptical. 'How you know?'

Crowe looked at him disdainfully. 'You figure yourself for a fighter, Montana, but you're not even a decent brawler. This Cade is a real fighter.'

Montana frowned at Crowe. 'Mebbe we'll find out sometime, you an' me, but how you know about Cade?'

'Seen him before. He was bare-knuckle champ of 'A' Troop, First Wind River Cavalry — ' He stopped speaking suddenly, and grabbed Montana by his upper arm, not realizing how tightly he was gripping. The man yelled and tried to struggle free as Crowe said, 'See? Told you he'd — Aaah! Smart move! No uppercut — that could bust your knuckles, too — you watch this.' Cade hit Casey in the plexus, and when the big man jack-knifed — '*There!*' yelled Crowe excitedly. 'Told you! Used his knee, then clubbed his fist and hammered Casey on the back of the neck! Smart fightin'. Too smart for a dumb bastard like Casey.'

'Leggo my arm, Crowe! Hell, man, you grip hard! You seem to know a lot about this damn sheriff.'

Crowe nodded, watching Cade lean-ing on the bar, getting back his breath, fists clenched at his sides as he stood over the unconscious Casey.

'Yeah, I know him now . . . Just wonder how the judge is gonna take it when I tell him who we got for sheriff!'

Montana grunted. 'He ain't so tough. Casey was half drunk. Hey, Cade!' Chris turned his head, wiping blood from his mouth, finding Montana, but not speaking. 'I'd kill any man did that to me.'

Montana gestured to the sprawled Casey, tensed involuntarily as he met Cade's steely stare.

'Me too,' Chris told him flatly and picked up the glass of whiskey Burl had already poured him. He downed it like a man who not only needed it, but had damn well earned it — the hard way.

★ ★ ★

Judge Kirk looked at Crowe steadily, standing in the front doorway of his house, clutching a table napkin. Obviously he had been disturbed at dinner, and didn't like it.

'Casey didn't do as he was told?'

Crowe smiled crookedly. 'Not for want of tryin', Judge. Cade was just too good for him. Too good for a lot of men.'

'You included, I take it? You being a man with a pugilistic background, that you and Cade have, er, met within the roped square at some time?'

Crow sobered. 'Never had the chance. Names were drawed out of a hat, and we never matched up.'

'But you'd like to see if you could beat him, wouldn't you?'

'Mebbe. Long time since I've gone twenty rounds. Once went open-ended. That's when we had to keep fightin' 'til one of us dropped. Feller I was up against collapsed at round thirty.' He grinned tightly. 'About ten seconds later, I joined him on the mat, but I was declared winner.'

'We may . . . arrange something for

you with Cade, if Casey doesn't finish the job he was paid to do.'

Crowe frowned. 'You're givin' him another chance?'

The judge held up a hand, the one with the napkin, and dabbed at his lips before replying. 'He ought to be good and mad now. Don't try to hold him back. Just make sure he doesn't incur any more injuries by getting too close to Cade. You understand?'

Crowe pursed his scarred lips. 'Kinda drastic at this stage, ain't it?'

'*Do — you — understand?*'

'Yeah, yeah,' Crowe said slowly. 'Just that I don't think — '

'You don't have to!' Kirk cut in edgily. 'I'll do the thinking for you. Now go arrange things. I have dinner guests waiting.'

He slammed the door in Crowe's face and the big man let out a long breath, walked back down the path through the judge's garden to the gate.

He did not look happy.

* * *

Cade washed up in his room, leaning his hands on the small table and letting the blood-tinged water run off his face, before sluicing more over the swellings and one graze. He worked his jaw slowly and cautiously. It hurt and he thought the tooth socket was bleeding again. His head was still ringing from that heavy blow of Casey's and for a moment he wished he'd locked Casey up, but figured it was better if he left it as a private deal and didn't throw his weight around too much as a lawman at this stage.

Whether it would buy him anything he wasn't sure, but Casey was going to be a sick-and-sorry man for a while.

He spun swiftly, Colt whispering out of leather into his hand as the door opened and Wiley stepped in, stopping dead when she saw the gun.

'My God! That was *fast*!'

'Used to have fast-draw contests just for the hell of it when I was in the army.

You got a bad habit of not knocking first, Wiley.'

As he holstered the gun she closed the door and came in carrying a small drawstring calico bag which she held up. 'Thought I might play nursemaid.'

'Ain't gonna argue with you.'

She motioned to the bed and he sat down on the edge. She took bandages and a couple of bottles of lotion from the bag and went to work gently on his battered face.

'You look awful, but not as bad as Casey.'

'He gone?'

'Couple of the swampers carried him out back to the lean-to Burl keeps for his friends.' She smiled. 'Let's them sober up before they have to go face their wives.'

Cade nodded and sat there while she cleaned up his wounds. 'Burl send you up?'

She snapped her head up and there was a brief blaze in her blue eyes. 'It was my own idea.'

He realized he had hurt her by the question but didn't know just how to smoothe things out, except to mutter, 'Well . . . I'm glad to see you, Wiley.'

She said nothing, but she was tight-lipped now as she finished up, gathering her things, dropping the blood-tinged rags into the basin of water.

'I'll get rid of this . . . '

'I can do it,' he said as she lifted it but knew instantly it was the wrong thing. 'Yeah, sure. Thanks, Wiley. I won't forget this.'

Her face softened a little. 'Maybe I'll give you a chance later to prove that — if you're feeling fit enough.'

'It's my face that took the beatin'.'

She smiled then, went to the narrow back door and juggled the basin trying to keep it from spilling while she fumbled at the door. 'It's locked . . . '

'Just me bein' careful,' Cade said as he strode across, turned the key, pulled the door open and stepped back. 'If you have time later, we — '

She screamed and threw the basin of bloody water from her as Cade glimpsed a movement out on that narrow balcony: a man crouching, lifting an instinctive arm across his face as the water hit him. He triggered the gun in his other fist.

Wiley shuddered and was slammed back into Cade as he lunged forward, Colt sliding into his hand. He caught her round the waist with his left arm, her slumping weight pulling him off-balance, causing the second bullet meant for him to gouge splinters from the door, as his own Colt bucked and roared in his fist.

The man out there in the dark, just beyond the reach of the weak light from the room's single lamp, reared up with the striking lead, crashed through the thin rail and plummeted down into the alley, bouncing off the sloping roof of the old lean-to at the rear of the saloon.

Cade knew it was Casey, and he was either dead or unconscious: he'd have a bunch of broken bones, for sure. *The more the merrier!* Cade didn't care about him.

Wiley was his immediate concern and he lifted her gently on to the bed as boots clattered up the stairs from the saloon and the door burst open. A man in range clothes he didn't know stood there, blinking. Cade snapped his head around. 'Get a sawbones! *Pronto!*'

The man tried to turn and do as ordered but the crush of gawkers was too much. Swearing, Cade drew his Colt and put a bullet into the ceiling. The mob cleared as everyone sought cover and the sheriff yelled,

'Only the sawbones gets in!'

'Hey, Chris! C'mon, feller, what the hell happened?'

It was Burl Randall, shoving and jostling his way into the room. Cade holstered the gun. 'Casey was waiting on the balcony. Sonuver's dead, I think — don't much care one way or t'other. Wiley saved my neck.' He raised his voice. 'Where's that damn doctor?'

A man with a black bag and no coat

over his shirt arrived within the next five minutes and Cade, who had been holding a cloth pressed against the bleeding wound in Wiley's side, snapped,

'About time! She was shot — ' Then he stared, surprised. '*You're* the sawbones . . . ?'

'Looks like it, doesn't it?' growled an irritable Shelby Hawkins. 'Now get out of the way so I can work.' He was already opening the bag. 'Someone fetch some hot water — and clear the room!'

Cade soon got the stickybeaks out and Randall ushered in the Indian woman who had brought Cade's bath water earlier. She had a pail of hot water and set it down beside the doctor, looked at the bloody wound where Wiley's dress had been ripped aside. She surprised Cade by crossing herself. Then she took a small wooden crucifix on a thong from inside her dress and held it tightly, turning from Wiley, lips moving in some prayer as she went out.

Christian Indians were not common and Cade, not a religious man himself, nonetheless hoped the prayer would help Wiley. 'How bad is it, Doc?'

'I'll know in a minute. The bullet passed right through, between the ribs. I don't think there's any organ damage. Maybe a bone chipped . . . '

'Is she gonna make it?'

'She's lost a good deal of blood and — '

'*Is she gonna make it?*'

Hawkins narrowed his eyes, recognized Cade's genuine concern, spoke calmly. 'I'll let you know. It'll be better if we don't move her, I think.'

'Then leave her be and do your best.'

Then Burl Randall came in through the back door. He had gone down the balcony stairs to the alley where a small crowd of drinkers had gathered around Casey's sprawled body.

'Casey's still breathin', but only just. Coupla fellers are takin' him to your infirmary, Doc.' He turned towards Cade. 'You got him alongside the head,

Chris. Damn good shootin', considerin'.'

'Not good enough,' Cade said, reloading his gun now as he watched the doctor work over Wiley.

She looked very white and the bed was heavily stained with her blood.

He wondered if it had been Casey's own idea to try to kill him, or if someone had planted the notion in his thick head . . . ?

He would find out and then maybe there would be a lot more shooting in Reno Creek . . .

Shelby Hawkins stood, wiped some beads of sweat from his brow. 'On second thoughts, I think I'd better move her to my infirmary. I'll arrange that and then take a look at Casey.'

'Make sure you give Wiley preference, Doc.'

Hawkins looked steadily at the sheriff. 'Have I told you how to do your job?'

Cade shrugged. 'She saved my life.'

Hawkins frowned, hesitated and then

nodded. 'Don't worry, I'll save hers. If it was you lying there, I might not be so concerned.'

'Careful, Doc — Your Hypercratic Oath's showin' . . . '

Hawkins glanced up sharply, eyes narrowed. 'You're pretty damn ruthless, aren't you? And a bit of a bastard thrown in.'

Cade spread his arms with a wry smile.

'What you see is what you get.'

Shelby Hawkins almost smiled.

'Yes. And I think that's surprising quite a few people in Reno Creek.' As he picked up his bag he added, 'Myself included.'

5

Mistakes

'Turnin' Casey loose on Cade was a mistake, Judge, that's all. It won't come to nothin'.'

Ethan Kirk turned from watching the movement on the dark street through the window, and glared at Crowe, sprawled in a chair at one end of Kirk's glass-enclosed porch. Apparently his dinner guests had left now but the judge's mood hadn't improved.

'I'm hoping that mistake won't be compounded by someone finding more money on Casey than he could be expected to have . . . thanks to you.'

Crowe, just lighting a cigarette he had rolled, paused, pulling his head back so it wasn't too brightly illuminated by the match.

'You just said pay him — not when.

He wouldn't've done it anyway without seein' the money.'

'Goddamnit, Crowe! You could've given him a small down payment.'

Crowe shrugged, lit the cigarette and exhaled. 'No use worryin'. Some of the fellers gathered round him lyin' in the alley might've cleaned out his pockets anyway — happens all the time — and Casey had no friends.' Crowe hesitated. 'I hear there's a good chance he won't make it.'

'I'd be happier if we could be sure of that.'

'Aw, no. Don't say what I think you're thinkin', I won't go near that infirmary and no way can you ask Shelby Hawkins to just let him die, so I'd forget it and just hope he don't make it.'

'You're a bearer of nothing but bad news!'

'Judge, there's nothin' you can do about Casey right now. Just have to wait 'n' see what happens.'

The judge glared at Crowe through

the darkness and then made an obvious effort to relax.

'Nothin' Casey can say, anyway, Judge. He claims he was paid to shoot Cade, but who's gonna believe him? He's such a vindictive sonuver, holds a grudge for years — everyone knows that, and the town'll just figure he was bein' his usual ornery self because Cade gave him a lickin' — for the second time.'

'Ye-es. If only that damn saloon girl hadn't got in the way. She's popular and will keep a lot of attention focused on this.'

'Latest word is she'll pull through OK.' Crowe stood. 'I wouldn't lose any sleep over this, Judge. It was just a simple mistake.'

'With Casey, yes. Unfortunately, we made a much bigger mistake, misjudging Chris Cade . . . He could cost us the whole deal. We might have to send Montana out into the basin and stir things up enough so Cade'll have to go look into it . . . along those dangerous trails . . . '

Crowe pursed his lips. 'Montana's none too smart.'

'But he does what he's told.' The judge looked coldly at Crowe who heaved a sigh as he stood and nodded, adjusting his hat. 'Now, go see what you can find out.'

'You're the boss.'

* * *

Shelby Hawkins's face was drawn, etched with strain and fatigue, when Chris Cade opened the door of his room, gun in hand. It was very late and the saloon was quiet. Cade tensed.

'Good or bad news, Doc?' He stepped aside, ushering the weary medic in, and turning up the lamp as Hawkins slumped into a chair. 'Drink?'

Hawkins lifted a hand and let it drop back on to his knee. 'I think I'd pass out on the spot. I'll leave the drink till I get back home and then I can fall into bed straight after.'

Cade sat on the edge of the bed, gun

dangling from his hand. Hawkins managed a wan smile.

'You're a careful man, Cade.'

'How's Wiley, Doc?'

'She's going to be all right. It'll take some time, but she's heathy and will pull through. I had to operate to repair a little internal damage, but yes, she'll live. I don't expect any complications.'

'That's all I wanted to hear.'

'I borrowed Payne's dental gas for the operation — it's gentler than chloroform. They invariably vomit with chloroform and I didn't want her convulsing with that wound . . . I also have news about Casey.'

Cade gave him a direct look. 'I ain't really interested, Shelby. Whatever happens to him, he deserves, far as I'm concerned. The stupid sonuver tried to kill me.'

Hawkins gave him a steady look, didn't answer right away. 'Yes, and may have been paid to do so.' He reached into his pocket and brought out a thin wad of notes. 'I've never known Casey to have so much money on him. He was always bullying someone to pay for his drinks and it was rumoured he rolled drunks.' He held out the money to Cade. 'This was in his pocket — a little blood on it, which may be appropriate.'

Cade counted quickly, looked up, smiling wryly. 'Hell, I'm only worth a hundred bucks. In keeping with that cheapskate town council though, especially the judge.'

'I wouldn't care to hazard a guess about where it came from. You should be grateful Casey wasn't successful.'

'Thanks to Wiley.' Cade tossed the money on the bedside table and snorted. 'Is Casey really dying?'

'He probably won't make it through the night.' Frowning, Shelby lowered his eyes, studying his slim hands that seemed to Cade to tremble slightly. 'Not because of your bullet, but rather the broken bones from his fall. His lung may be punctured and perhaps even the aorta is damaged.'

He paused and watched Cade whose

face didn't change expression. 'I'm hardly in a position to be calling you callous, Chris — I'm just as guilty: I gave Casey a whiff of that dental gas, recalling how you talked about yourself while you were under its influence . . . I questioned him.'

He paused as Cade stared and gave a faint smile. 'Well, you must've been in a reckless mood.'

The doctor scowled. 'Surprisingly, I accomplished what I set out to do. I may've led Casey to believe that he would not survive the night, so he'd be more willing to talk.'

He paused but Cade merely looked at him with a carefully composed face.

'Well, wanting, no doubt, to clear his conscience, Casey admitted he was the one who threw the fire-cracker under the horse that killed my brother.'

Cade waited, said somewhat impatiently, 'And . . . ?'

'A man named Brick Duggan was the stallion's rider, and supposedly so upset about the incident that immediately afterwards he quit Magruder's and left the county.'

'Was the horse his? The stallion, I mean.'

'I assumed it was one of Magruder's remuda.'

'Uh-huh. Who broke the stallion in?'

'Magruder's wrangler, I suppose.'

'You know anything about this Duggan?'

'Not much. He just turned up at Padlock and Magruder gave him a job. He didn't have *quite* the look of a cowhand but he was rugged enough, I suppose, and must've known his job or Pat Magruder wouldn't've kept him on: I heard he was very disturbed by Mel's death . . . ' He paused again. 'And apparently he's still around.'

'Thought you just said he left the county . . . ?'

'Oh, Duggan quit, all right, or he was paid off. But, according to Casey, he's living back in the hills with Padlock's wrangler — Mustang someone-or-other who — '

Cade was very tense now, spoke quietly. 'Mustang McLeary . . . ? Was he Magruder's wrangler?'

'I think so. What's wrong?' He tensed at the sudden cold expression on Cade's face. 'The name means something to you . . . ?'

Cade nodded, voice tense. 'I know McLeary — animal hater. People hater, too. He's been known to train dogs to turn on their owners when he gives some special command. It's rumoured that once he trained a horse especially to kill a woman who ripped his face up when he tried to rape her. He went to jail for two years for the rape, and she was trampled to death soon after his release. He's got a long memory, never forgives.'

Hawkins was on his feet by now. 'He trained a horse to kill on command?'

Cade nodded. 'So they say. It reacted to some kinda signal he'd taught it . . . and I'll bet that poor damn animal suffered plenty before Mustang was satisfied.'

'My God! He — he could've prepared that stallion to react to the fire crackers and — '

'Sounds like a good bet, Shelby. Mustang's three parts Indian, the rest unadulterated rattler.' He went quiet, saw Hawkins frowning at something in his tone, then added, 'If he had some grudge against your brother, he just could've fixed it. He thrives on hate, for men or animals. And some of that could be blamed on me.' He drew down a deep breath.

'It happened a couple years ago . . .'

Chris was point rider and scout for Boss Fredericks's herd, coming up from the Cimarron and heading for Dodge City. There were nigh on seven thousand head in the herd and they were denuding the trail at a fast rate because the season had been drier than expected, grass short and far from nutritious.

After Coldwater, the situation was heading towards crisis level and Fredericks rode out to see Cade who had climbed to a vantage point on a hogback rise from where he could see what lay ahead.

Fredericks was a big, squared-headed Swede, actually born in Denmark, but 'Swede' covered a lot of territory when used by a cowhand. 'Boss' had some kind of accent and he was as hard a man as Cade had ever seen riding the cattle trails. But he was scrupulously fair, morally stable and expected the same from his men when driving herd. Once they hit a trail town, OK: one night was theirs to do with what they wanted.

But next day, any man who didn't front up or work as he should, found a scrap of paper thrust into his pocket that bore the precise money he was owed and could be collected from any Cattleman's Bank on Fredericks's signature. This was followed by one mighty swipe across the side of the head, knocking the poor, hungover fool clear out of the saddle.

'I give you — an' gladly — freedom for one good time. You give me nothin' but moans an' groans so you no good to me. Now ride over yonder ridge by the time I counta twenty or you have to out-run my bullet.'

Every man who left Fredericks's herd that way, spurred and lashed their mounts in a wind-burning flight to the hills.

One of these was Mustang McLeary.

Boss caught him whipping one of the remuda with a knotted rope end, took it away from the startled breed and smashed him across the head, knocking him senseless.

'Chris, you going to cross the badlands, see what feed is like. Take this dung with you. Make sure he dunna come back.'

Chris Cade didn't like it. He wanted nothing to do with Mustang, had seen his methods working the remuda and had once threatened to shoot him if he didn't treat the animals with more care. Mustang had said nothing but the smouldering look of hatred in those dark eyes gave Chris a sensation of goosebumps rippling all over his body.

But Fredericks had to be obeyed . . .

There was a dust storm and they got lost. It took until midday, almost twenty-four hours after it had started, before it began to clear. They found themselves in really bad country, little grass and the crumbling sun-baked rocks warned Cade there was not much chance of finding sweet water.

Then a war party of Kiowa found them and forced them deeper into the badlands. They rode fast, shot straight and when the pursuit finally gave up, Cade knew they were in real trouble: if the local renegades wouldn't tackle this desolate stretch it must be really bad . . .

Their horses were near jaded from the long hard-riding chase. They had shot four Kiowa — Mustang had scalped them all — and Cade had caught an arrow in the left thigh. His horse was in better condition than Mustang's and the breed, instead of acknowledging that his mount was faltering, kicked and spurred and beat it about the head until, finally, it veered off a ledge, rolled on top of him and snapped a foreleg when it jammed between two rocks.

Mustang picked himself up out of the dust, swearing, wiping blood from his nostrils, one ear also bleeding. He strode back to the floundering horse and began to kick it about the head and neck.

'Cut that out!' snapped Cade, drawing his gun. 'You blamed idiot, it's done its best for you. Show it some consideration, then we'll have to ride double and hope my mount can get us out of here.'

Mustang grunted and walked across. 'Take your foot outta the stirrup while I swing aboard.'

Cade took his boot out of the stirrup but kicked the breed in the head sending him staggering. He was a medium sized man, very hard-muscled, and his tribal pigtails and swarthy skin, now bloody and sweat-streaked, gave him a mighty mean look as his dark eyes blazed.

'The hell you doin'!' he exploded.

Cade threw down with his gun as Mustang reached for his own weapon. 'You're not riding with me until you put that poor damn horse out of its misery!'

Mustang frowned, looked at the whinnying mount and its broken leg, the bone showing through the torn skin, as it fought futilely to get up, grunting and whickering in pain.

'That damn crowbait? It's fought me every inch of the way! I never had one lousy minute of comfort in the saddle! I'm the one had the misery — now it's his turn.'

'You son of a bitch! Put a bullet in that horse's head and give it some peace, or I'll damn well put one in you.'

Mustang tensed. 'Don't push it, Cade! I don' like you, never have nor never will. Mebbe this is the place to do somethin' about it.'

'Mebbe, but first, give that horse the

quick death it deserves.' The animal's pathetic whickering and struggles were making Cade mighty edgy. He hated seeing any animal suffer.

Mustang laughed harshly. 'You're so worried about it bein' in pain, use one of your own bullets!'

Chris looked hard at the man with his dust reddened eyes, bulging a little with the man's fury. A minute passed in the blazing sun, the tail end of the dust storm rasping at his nostrils and throat, stinging his eyes.

He suddenly hipped in the saddle and fired into the injured horse's head. It jerked and thrashed briefly, then was still.

Mustang hawked and spat and moved forward, reaching for the saddle to swing up behind Chris. 'OK, let's get the hell outta here.'

Cade planted a boot against his chest and shoved him back roughly. Mustang swore, floundering. He reached for his gun, then screamed as Cade shot him in the left foot, the bullet ripping open the buckskin of the moccasin Mustang habitually wore, splintered bone erupting, blood spurting. He fell backwards, rolling and thrashing, knee bent as he tried to reach the mangled foot.

He sobbed and moaned, huddled, staring up at Chris, his face contorted. 'You . . . *bastard!*'

'See how you like crossin' the badlands with a busted leg. You might get some notion of what that hoss would've gone through.'

Mustang was spitting an endless stream of invective but suddenly stopped as Chris wheeled his mount and started to ride away.

'Jesus! You can't leave me here!'

'Crawl or walk — it's not far, only about ten, twelve miles. Could be twenty but I doubt that. Do you good to suffer a mite, like every poor damn animal you've ever handled.'

'I-I got no water!'

'Sure you have. Your canteen's still on your horse — only thing is now he's lying on it. You'll need to dig under him to get it.'

'Why — why you doin' this to me?'

'You figure it out. No one's gonna miss you if you don't make it, Mustang. Live with that thought a while — then die with it. Look on the bright side: you might find that wagonload of gold that's s'posed to have disapppeared into thin air out this way. Then you can die rich.'

Chris spurred away and Mustang fought to get his gun free of the holster. By the time he did, Cade had ridden over the next rise and the four shots the breed triggered in frustrated anger were wasted . . .

'Never lost a minute's sleep over leavin' Mustang. Heard a year ago he was still looking for me but nothing ever came of it. Made a mistake, though. I'll be looking over my shoulder for the rest of my life unless we get it settled.'

Shelby Hawkins was staring, his mouth slightly open.

'You're much tougher than I thought, Chris. But, now what? Will you bring Duggan back?'

'If he's there.'

'And — Mustang?'

'Up to him.'

6

Directions

It was raining, though not heavily, when Chris stopped by the infirmary to see Wiley.

She was awake, but still slightly groggy from the gas and whatever medication Shelby had given her. She looked pale and he could tell it hurt her to move as she winced and grimaced, edging around so she could face him better beside the bed.

'I — thought the rain had — stopped?'

'Just about,' he said draping his damp slicker over one arm. 'But I've got a ride to make. How you feeling?'

'Don't really know. My head's all muzzy and my side hurts.'

'Hawkins says you're on the way to recovery.'

She smiled wanly. 'Well, if he also said it's a slow, painful process, I'll believe him.'

'Good to see you haven't lost your sense of humour.'

She looked up at him, then a small frown appeared on her brow as she studied him from head to foot. 'You're going somewhere?'

'Just up into the hills, I think.' At her quizzical look he added, 'Looking for a cabin somewhere back of Magruder's.'

'A cabin? Well, I know he still has an old lineshack up there, but he hasn't used it for a long time. It was too far from the ranch so he built another, closer in. I think he stores some tools in the original place and a little canned food in case some puncher gets caught out and needs shelter there for the night.'

'Sounds like a good-thinkin' range man.'

She frowned slightly. 'He's hard, a partner with Kirk in the ranch, but they say he's a very good cattleman.'

He waited for more and she smiled slightly.

'I know about the lineshack because once or twice Magruder hired it out to a couple of married men from town who wanted to . . . meet me.'

He kept his face straight, reminding himself of Wiley's profession, and nodded. 'Looking for a feller named Duggan, s'posed to be staying with a wrangler called Mustang Mc — '

'Leary!' she finished for him and grimaced as she made a sudden grab at her side. 'I'm all right. Moved too fast, that's all.'

'You know Mustang?'

'Know him! I'd like to castrate him!' She shuddered. 'I refused to take him as a customer one time. He felt insulted, kidnapped me and took me to that lineshack.' She grimaced again, but not in pain — only painful memories. 'The bastard had all kinds of ugly hell planned for me, but I managed to knock him out with a poker and got away.'

'Who was sheriff then?'

She laughed shortly. 'The one before Mel Hawkins — useless drunk — so Mustang got away with it. Burl wouldn't even allow him in the saloon after that. You'd do well to stay away from that son of a bitch, Chris.'

'I have to see Duggan, which means I have to get past Mustang. We're kind of overdue for a squarin'-off, anyway.'

She sucked in a sharp breath. 'My God! You be damn careful!'

'I aim to be. But first I need to find him.'

He looked at her meaningfully and she shook her head.

'I — I don't want to tell you . . . I don't want you to tangle with that snake.'

'I'll go ask Magruder then, or someone. But I have to get to Duggan, Wiley.'

'Brick Duggan? What's so important about him? He's only some two-bit engineer down on his luck. Magruder gave him a riding job just so he could make a living.'

'How d'you know he's an engineer?'

She smiled. 'In my job, Chris, you get to hear all kinds of things — what some men will tell you! I'm well past my blushing days but once in a while my hair stands on end.'

He smiled. 'Be somethin' to see. What kind of engineer?'

Her eyes narrowed. 'You're persistent, aren't you?'

He said nothing, and she sighed. 'Don't really know. Wasn't that interested. I might have it wrong, he could be a surveyor, in that line. But he sure was no ranch-hand, said once he'd be glad when he could come out in the open and stop playing at being a cowboy . . .'

'Sounds like someone didn't want it known what he really was. I do have to find him, Wiley — it's important.'

She tightened her lips until they were bloodless, still shaking her head. 'No! I won't tell you how to get to that shack, it's too dangerous.' He continued to look and then she sighed. 'Oh, damn you!'

'You're too late — I've been damned by experts.'

So, in the end she told him how to find the remote lineshack and he was on the trail, riding through driving rain, in under an hour.

* * *

The rain was heavier than he expected and the first creek was already frothing and running a banker.

He rode upstream, hoping to find a shallower or narrower place to cross and after a mile or so was able to swim his reluctant mount over. The current was fierce even though the water level was just under the gelding's belly and he had a fight on his hands. But the animal trusted him and heaved out safely on the far bank.

He had ridden only another four hundred yards before he realized he was on a low hogback, separating the flooding creek from a wide, saucer-shaped basin. Muddy water streamed down the slopes into the basin and already there was a sizeable lake of mud-coloured water, rising gradually. If it rained for a few days, this would flood over into the creek to make it even bigger.

And if that joined up with the Arkansas River, there'd be a lake lapping the outskirts of Dodge City itself.

He shook himself abruptly, wondering how his mind had jumped in that direction so quickly, but it sure as hell was raining like the first of the forty days and nights as described in the Bible.

The horse was still shaking from the crossing as he rode north-west along the ridge of the hogback, seeing where it sloped away from the basin a little farther along.

The horse seemed much more controllable so he guessed he had picked the right direction.

Going down the far slope of the hogback where it petered out and lost itself in the surrounding country, he came to a fork in the trail which was appearing again: he must have cut across the long curving loop he had been expecting, likely hidden by the flooding water, then picked up the trail again that he had been following originally.

Luck, plain luck . . .

He hoped it would hold and when he came to the dripping signpost with a few weathered boards nailed on to it, pointing in several directions, he figured his luck was indeed holding.

These were the names and distances of the various spreads: Padlock (2 miles); Box 7(5½ miles); Square 4 (10 miles); Arrowhead (7 miles) — but pointing in a different direction to the others — and three more he didn't bother to read.

But only two miles from Padlock . . . it was too tempting to pass up.

He swung the smoke gelding towards the beginning of the trail that would eventually lead him to Magruder's.

The trail was muddy and there were two washaways, but easy enough to negotiate. He paused under a tree on a low ridge, the rain easing some now. Using his slicker for protection, he rolled a lumpy cigarette. He managed to get it burning as he looked at the ranch, kind of misty through the still slanting rain.

A big ranch house and two bunkhouses, one long, the other about half the size. Four large corrals, two back-to-back barns, a feature you didn't often see this far south, but common enough in the Big Sky country up north.

There must be forty-odd horses in those corrals, plus whatever others were out on the range working the cattle herds. Padlock was a big spread, a going concern, and he figured —

'You're on private land here, mister,' a voice said behind him suddenly, startling him. He dropped the damp cigarette, at the same time sweeping back the slicker folds to clear his gun rig.

Hipping slowly, he saw the rider in a patched brown poncho beside a second tree with a thicker trunk than the one he was sheltering beneath. The man held a Winchester carbine in his hands, thumb on the hammer spur.

At least it wasn't cocked — yet.

'Ease off, *amigo*, I'm Sheriff Cade from Reno Creek.'

He pushed the slicker aside some more so the man could see the badge. The gun didn't move and Chris studied the rider: stubbled, mud-streaked, worn boots with blunted spur rowels, leather chaps, short in the saddle. *Cowhand, not a special guard, just sheltering from the rain.*

'Heard about you. You headin' in to the house?'

'Is Magruder there?'

The man nodded and suddenly sheathed the carbine in the saddle

104

scabbard. 'I'll ride down with you. They call me 'Stretch'.'

Standing, he wouldn't've reached Cade's shoulder. Chris looked at him sharply but the narrow face was unsmiling. 'I can see why,' he said flatly.

Then Stretch grinned. 'Just as well I'm easy-goin' or I'd be fightin' day and night.'

'Just as well. You know Brick Duggan?'

The grin faded. 'Not too well. Kept to himself, spent a lot of time up at the house with the boss.'

'Unusual.'

'Magruder's business, I reckon.'

Cade nodded and they were mostly silent on the remainder of the ride down to the house. They stopped at the first and smallest corral and Stretch swung down quickly.

'Best you wait here till I see the boss. Standin' orders: visitors wait till announced. Rain's not too bad right now. Someone'll look after you.'

He hurried inside and Montana

came out a few minutes later, hatless, stopping on the porch and motioning Cade to come on up. He gave Cade the once-over before leading the way inside. The floor was covered in polished linoleum. Curtly, Montana made the introductions in a very masculine parlour. The walls were dotted with antler racks of varying sizes, all worthy of the record books, two mounted stag heads, and one buffalo head, dominating the south wall.

Pat Magruder was a wiry man in his fifties, grey in his short hair and drooping moustache, weathered face tanned dark as a rifle butt, deeply etched with crows' feet and lines around his mouth and across his forehead. The eyes were watchful and probing. He studied Chris openly, then abruptly thrust out his right hand. It was bony and gnarled from years of ranch work, firm and welcoming.

'Lousy day for such a long ride from town, Sheriff.'

'Was heading elsewhere when I came

across the sign-post. Figured another couple miles wouldn't hurt — was already half-drowned.'

Magruder nodded. 'Coffee or whiskey?'

Chris pointed to the decanter on a polished side table and the rancher nodded to Montana who silently poured two slugs into glasses that glittered so much Cade figured they must be crystal. Montana did not pour a drink for himself though he looked like he wanted to. Magruder and Cade raised their glasses in a silent toast and sipped.

'Man, that hits the spot!'

'Import it from Ireland, the real stuff. So you're the judge's new man.'

Cade's gaze was steady over the rim of the glass. 'No, I'm the new sheriff of Reno Creek.'

'He's his own man, he says,' Montana dropped in.

Magruder moved his head a little, jaw jutting. He watched Cade as he sipped more whiskey. 'Not sure Ethan

Kirk'll like that attitude.'

'He knows — now.'

The rancher nodded slowly. 'Bet he was surprised, and not necessarily pleased.' He tossed down the rest of his drink. 'You said you were headed someplace else.' Magruder gestured briefly towards a window without looking. 'Big country out there. Not a lot of places a man'd want to go. 'Specially in this kinda weather.'

Cade smiled thinly at the barely disguised probing.

'Not that I want to go, more a case of have to. You might help. I'm looking for one of your old linecamps.'

Montana stiffened. Nothing obviously changed in Magruder's stance or looks, but there was some sort of subtle shifting in the eyes. 'Only got but one. Had a couple more but pulled 'em down. Likely do the same to this last one. Serves no useful purpose. Why you looking for it?'

Cade drained his glass, shook his head when the rancher gestured to the whiskey bottle. 'That'll hold me, thanks. Heard Brick Duggan's up there.'

This time Magruder was noticeably startled by the lawman's sudden admission. He glanced sharply at Montana, held out his glass, and the foreman poured a generous slug of the rich whiskey for his boss.

'Duggan? Well, he worked for me for a short time. Actually gave him a job 'cause I felt sorry for him. Fiddlefooted, couldn't punch cows worth a damn.'

'No experience?'

'Not much. Dunno what he really worked at but he was solidly built, had the outdoor look. Tell the truth I was kinda disappointed when he turned out to be no good, but I had to let him go.'

'He was no loss,' opined Montana.

'You should've chosen a better horse for him to ride in that race a few weeks back, in Reno Creek. You recall?'

Magruder's hard eyes glittered now. 'Of course I damn well recall! What the hell're you playing at? You gonna make some trouble over what happened to Mel Hawkins? 'Cause if you are, you can forget it. Damn hoss was spooky, and some idiot tossed a firecracker under it, sent it loco.'

'And Duggan couldn't control it, and before you knew it, it'd stomped Mel Hawkins into the ground.'

Magruder's face pinched as he nodded slowly. 'You've got it. Poor old Duggan got throwed but the hurts he got from that didn't bother him half as much as how bad he felt about not bein' able to stop the horse from killing Mel.'

'A man with a conscience.' Montana tensed a little at the look Magruder threw him: *maybe he better shut up . . .*

'Seems to me if you figured he was such a lousy rider you shouldn't've let him enter the Reno race at all.'

'How could I stop him? I'd given him his time, told him he could work out the week. He had his eye on the prize money, I guess, something to ride out with.'

Cade nodded thoughtfully. 'Never thought of that angle. You know who threw that firecracker?' When the rancher shook his head irritably, Cade said, 'It was Bull Casey — told Doc Hawkins he had the cracker stuffed into a cheroot so no one'd see it. He lit it up and when it burned down enough to reach the short wick, he dropped it under Duggan's horse then disappeared into the crowd, I guess.'

Magruder composed his face into deadpan lines, but couldn't disguise his sudden interest in Cade. 'Casey never did have any brains. You been investigating already?'

'Picked up a few things here and there, includin' how Duggan disappeared right after the . . . accident.'

'He quit! Right there and then. Poor devil was all shook up, couldn't accept that there was no blame on him. He was a mess, wasn't he, Montana?'

'And then some, boss. Really cut up about the whole deal. Just up an' quit an' — disappeared.'

'Not quite,' Cade said flatly.

Magruder made an impatient gesture. 'Just a figure of speech. Yeah, I heard he'd been seen over in Pratt County — that's two counties across from Ford here.'

'Long ways to hightail it when he had nothing to fear from the law.' Cade snapped his fingers. 'But the law in Ford County was dead by then, of course . . . '

Magruder's deepset eyes narrowed and the voice was quiet and unfriendly. 'Then you happened along, to stir up a hornets' nest out of an accident witnessed by hundreds of people! What're you playing at, Cade? Did Doc Hawkins put you up to this?'

Cade remained calm. 'A lawman was killed. Far as I can make out it was never investigated, no report made to the US marshal in the county seat at Kinlaw. I didn't ask for this job, Magruder, but I like to make a good fist of whatever work I take on. So I'm just checking the facts to make sure they're as they appear.'

The rancher remained coldly silent. Cade said, sounding casual, 'Just for interest, where'd you get the horse that killed Mel Hawkins? One of your own remuda? Or did you buy it from Mustang McLeary?'

'I don't do business with that breed.' Magruder walked over to the window, eased the drapes aside slightly. 'Rain's just about stopped.' He turned and faced the sheriff. 'Be a good time for you to get on your way, Cade, before it starts coming down heavy again. The trails around here can be dangerous. Mudslides and worse. Right, Montana?'

'Dead right, boss. Mighty dangerous, especially if you dunno 'em too well.' He locked his green gaze on Cade who remained stoical, held that drilling gaze a long moment, then nodded.

'Yeah, I got that impression, too. Well, mebbe you can tell me how to find this old linecamp. Least I can do is see if Duggan's there, and if he is, get a statement I can take to Kinlaw.'

'If you think it's necessary, I'll tell you how to find the old lineshack. Duggan won't be there, I'm sure of that. But you could shelter overnight. I leave a case of canned grub for any drifter who might stop by.'

He went to a desk and brought out a pad and pencil. 'I'll draw you a rough map. This here big X will be the ranch house, right? Then if you go back the way you came to the trees where Stretch found you, here, keep riding north with the main hills on your left.'

His voice droned on as he sketched in the trails he suggested Cade take. Montana left while they were studying the sketched map: Chris thought a look passed between the ramrod and Magruder — even had a notion as to what it meant.

Chris thanked Magruder for his trouble, and left.

But he had no intention of following the rancher's directions: they didn't even begin to match those given him by Wiley.

Magruder had deliberately misled him; if he followed the directions he'd just been given, he would end up nowhere near the real location of the lineshack.

Which meant he had better keep a watch on his backtrail — and damn closely at that.

7

Dead End Trail

He found his way back to the clump of trees where he had first met Stretch without any trouble, although the rain was getting heavier now. It drummed against his slicker, the constant stream of water from his hat brim making him shake his head so he could see better.

From this point he could find his way back to the signpost and then pick up the trail described by Wiley. He rode in under the big spread of branches that gave him some shelter, unsheathed his rifle and jacked a shell into the breech, lowering the hammer before sliding the weapon back into the wet leather.

He didn't care for riding with a load in the breech but it was theoretically safe with the hammer down. Many a time he had ridden with the rifle thus loaded and with the hammer back, in Indian country, when the danger was high and worth the risk to have a weapon ready for instant discharge if the red men attacked.

There was no use trying to smoke in this rain so he just made an effort to restrain his craving for tobacco and rode along the trail to the signpost. This was where Magruder's wrong directions started and he sat for a few moments in the shelter of a big boulder while he sorted out in his mind what Wiley had told him.

The trail was muddy, covered with inches of water, and when he reached the hogback above the basin, he saw that it was still filling with the run-off. He thought he glimpsed wet shingles on the slope above the water level: if someone was homesteading out there they must be watching that muddy water mighty closely, if the rain didn't ease, it could be soon lapping the doorstep of that nester's house.

He turned the smoke gelding on to

the trail he wanted and it took him into a boulder field where he stopped long enough to climb to the top of a flat-topped rock and squint along his backtrail.

No sign of any riders: they should be waiting beside the trail Magruder had wanted him to take. Still it didn't hurt to check.

He was wrong: Magruder had out-smarted him. Maybe he had sent men along the trails he had drawn on his pad in the ranch parlour, but he had used belt-and-braces caution, and posted at least one man along the correct trail.

Just in case . . .

First Cade knew of it was when a gunshot cracked, dulled by the rain, and a bullet chewed chips from the rock beside his head as he dropped into the saddle of the gelding. He fell forward on to the startled horse's neck and raked with his spurs.

The animal whinnied its protest but at the same instant lunged away and a second shot wasp-buzzed over Cade's head. *Damn fool marksman! Trying for a head-shot in these conditions!*

But luckily the man *was* making the difficult shot or he might be lying face down in the mud already, his last breaths bubbling the pooled slush . . .

Chris wheeled the mount aside, then wrenched the reins back, bringing more protests from the gelding but confusing the drygulcher. In desperation the man started shooting wildly, shot after shot, and by then Cade realized it was a carbine he was hearing, with that sudden, cut-off snap of a cracking whip, and not the booming of the longer-barrelled rifle.

Stretch had been carrying a carbine . . . . The thought flashed into his mind even as he glimpsed the spurt of smoke from another shot, the sound quickly dampened by the rain. The killer was on a ledge, a wall rising above him at his back, thinking it gave him protection.

It would have, normally, but not in rain this heavy. Even as Cade slid his

Winchester out of the scabbard and brought it up to his shoulder, knees gripping the running horse, he saw a sizeable slab of mud give way. It dropped on to the ledge close to the gunman, startled him so that he rolled on to his side and scrabbled out of the way.

It was Stretch, all right: not so easy-going after all, it seemed. Chris's rifle barked, his hand a blur as he levered and got off a second shot hard on the heels of the first. The lead clipped the jagged ledge and Stretch reared back instinctively, in time for the second shot to take him in the chest.

His small body jerked and he tumbled over, sliding down to end in a tangle about ten yards from where Chris sat his saddle. Cade jammed home the spurs and sent the horse veering left, just in time, as a bullet tore through the slack of his slicker: Stretch had not been alone.

He had been used as the distraction, though, and if he had been a better marksman he would have nailed the sheriff with his first or second shot.

Cade had ridden outlaw-infested trails for years and there weren't many snide tricks he didn't know about. So he stretched out along the smoke's back even as Stretch's body came to a standstill and, looking up under his dripping hatbrim, saw the movement behind a deadfall, not five yards ahead. A man rose to his knees, levering and shooting rapidly.

Cade triggered his rifle one-handed and threw himself out of the saddle on the far side of the racing horse. He twisted in midair, hit the slushy section of trail he had aimed for, slid out of control for a few yards and found himself within six feet of the deadfall. The rifleman was so close he had to stand up and lean over the log, in order to bead Cade.

But Chris's rifle lifted and blasted into his face.

The man slammed back out of sight and Cade grunted as his body thudded into the deadfall. He quickly kicked away from the log, rolled over and over and dropped into a depression half-filled with muddy water. He lay there, belly contracting as the cold water immediately soaked through his clothes, hands white and already wrinkled from the rain.

The sound of the gunshots had died quickly, muffled by the driving rain, which also would cover the sounds of any other riders closing in on the shooting. Cade's own horse had stopped down trail about twenty feet away, looking back curiously and with a mean eye at the treatment it had so recently received.

Cade lunged up and ran for it. The gelding hesitated, started to move away, but he grabbed the horn. His wet fingers slipped off and with a wild yell of effort he hurled himself bodily, leaping up so his arms went over the saddle. He clamped them tightly, still gripping the rifle, felt his boots wrenched free of the ground, then struggled and writhed until he managed to get astride the now running horse.

Once in the saddle properly, he held the reins in one hand, rifle in the other, gripped tightly with his knees and spoke calmly to the nervous mount. It soon settled and he raked his gaze over the trees and any high ground as they weaved along the trail.

When he broke out of the timber, he tensed: there was a rock-studded rise ahead which would be a good place for another drygulcher. He would have liked to take time to fully load the rifle — he didn't know how many cartridges were left in the magazine. But he wasn't prepared to slow down here and do it, and make a grand target for some ambusher.

He guided the horse around the base of the rise, his skin crawling between his shoulders, but no shots came. The spurs touched the wet flanks and the gelding increased its stride and pace. When the trail turned around a bluff he halted in the lee and let the mount pant and steam while he replenished the magazine with wet cartridges.

Sitting back, Winchester held barrel down to keep water out, his big hand tightly covering the open-top ejector port for the same reason, he took time to get his bearings. Wiley had described this bluff and had told him he needed to ride up a steep slope just beyond it. *Yes! He could see it ahead now!*

That would lead to a trail over that part of the range and Wiley said the lineshack was somewhere in the timber halfway up the slope of the mountain beyond — a long way from the Magruder ranch, all right. Probably it had been meant more as an out-camp just to secure his boundary so that he could hold all the land he was claiming at the time. It would have fallen into disuse after he settled his herds on the best pastures, closer to the main buildings.

It looked wild, undeveloped country up there, which meant there were plenty of hiding places to set up an ambush.

So he decided to skirt that first range instead of going up and over. It would be longer but, ultimately safer, he hoped.

He was dealing with desperate men here — he didn't know the *why* of it yet, but they were willing to kill so it was something big they were trying to cover up.

And he aimed to get to the bottom of it.

The rain hadn't eased much when he set the horse moving away from the bluff, heading north-east around the mountain.

He smelled woodsmoke on the damp air when he had been riding and zigzagging — *taking no chances* — for almost fifteen minutes. Halting the mud-spattered gelding, he tilted his head back, looked up the steep slope and saw one corner of what had to be the line-shack.

From here, Chris could make out a small corral with three horses standing drooping and miserable in the downpour. The cabin seemed to be in pretty good condition, maybe a couple of shingles missing here and there, but the walls were constructed of logs so it had been originally meant for permanency and would take a major effort to remove. Likely Magruder would simply burn it down — that's if he really did intend to demolish such a well-built structure.

He hadn't expected to see any sign of life and he didn't. It was just possible Duggan or Mustang — or both — had heard the shooting, but with the rain and two ranges between, it was just as possible that they hadn't.

Playing it safe, he worked on the presumption that the gunfire had been heard and suitable precautions had been taken.

Hopefully, if they were expecting him, or someone, they would be looking for him to approach from the other side of the mountain on the regular trail.

It was a steep climb and the gelding was weary, miserable in the rain: branches had scratched and torn its hide; the hard surface and stones underfoot had often given way as the ground softened, throwing its stride. He patted the wet head, those big, anxious eyes giving him fair warning not to push things too far . . .

Chris had always had good rapport with his mounts and this gelding was no exception. He grinned, despite his own tension, flipped one upright ear playfully, then led the animal into a sheltering pocket.

He took a handful of cartridges from his saddle-bags and filled his shirt pockets with them, then swigged from the canteen, although he had only to tilt up his face and open his mouth to let pure, cold rain run in, and he chided himself briefly for not thinking of that. After a final check of his six-gun he tugged down his sodden hat, and started up the steep muddy slope.

It was hard going and he fell several times, smothering the meaningless, instinctive curses that leapt to his lips. The slicker was confining, making his movements harder, but he didn't take it off. When he got closer he would shrug out of it, maybe, in case whoever was in the cabin heard the rustling of the stiff fabric.

Breathing was hard, the rain was so heavy, and he was a lot higher here now than when he had started out from Padlock. He was glad he hadn't tried to ride up: the horse would have taken many falls on the treacherous ground, might even have broken a leg.

He gave up trying to go straight up, the slope was simply too steep. So he started on a series of short zigzags, going left at a slight rising angle for ten yards, swinging back the other way, but still moving in a shallow climb, for five or six yards, or however far he felt able to manage easily. More than likely the approach on the front of the mountain was via a zigzag trail, too.

Cade made good progress this way and thought the rain was beginning to ease off. Then it would gust again with renewed violence and make him change his mind. But the steady downpour was breaking up into a series of showers, some heavier than others, so it was a sign the rain would eventually stop or become no more than a drizzle.

But he didn't want it to happen yet.

The noise of the heavier showers on the shingles would cover his falls which were becoming more frequent the higher he climbed. He rested behind some jutting boulders, only about fifty feet from the cabin now, and decided he would try the rear approach when he saw there was a door he hadn't noticed from down the slope. As he drew nearer he saw that it was made of sturdy planks and, if chained or on a good latch inside, would resist any assault he could make.

He might have to use the rifle to blast any lock away, but if it was just a simple drop-bar on the inside it would still beat him. Crouching, breath steaming, he ran his gaze along the peeled log wall closest to him. Two windows, but both with wooden shutters down. Well, he wouldn't have expected glass panes in a lineshack, anyway, but it would have been nice . . .

Now he had no choice: he had to go in from the front — and Mustang would be bound to have taken precautions. Or would he . . . ? With the back and side battened down, he might leave the front as a way out if he needed to run — any attacker would not be expecting that, would figure the escape route would be from the rear and concentrate his main force back there . . . leaving the front in the care of only a few guns. And if it was only a single man making the assault, Mustang would fight it out: he was no coward, whatever else he was.

He was not dumb, either, as Chris found out about one minute later when a voice behind him said,

'I don't believe it. I ain't usually a prayin' man but I sure as hell have prayed over the years to run into you again, Cade, you son of a bitch! Must be livin' right!'

Chris spun on to his back but froze as he started to bring his rifle around, encumbered by the stiff slicker.

Mustang was standing beside a tree he had obviously been hiding behind, a sawn-off shotgun held in both hands.

He was chuckling uncontrollably at his good luck in getting the drop on Cade, jerked the gun barrels in a short, lifting movement.

'Stay on your knees and hold the rifle by the muzzle — right at the end, damn you! OK, let the butt drag through the mud, then come on in, and *welcome*!'

He stepped behind Chris as the sheriff stumbled up the last few steep feet, limping badly on the left side. As he rammed the raw ends of the shotgun's barrel roughly against Chris's spine, making him stagger, the sheriff saw the twisted left foot that he had destroyed so long ago: it was a damn good bet that Mustang would be remembering, too . . .

'Man! I was gonna pull out after the rain stopped. Now I figure to spend a few more days here — and mighty pleasant days they gonna be.' He laughed loud, though briefly as he leaned down over Cade who had fallen forward. 'But not for you, Cade! Aw, hell no! *Not for you!*'

8

Linecamp

Inside the cabin it was gloomy, except for a dull glow from the stone fireplace at the far end. Cade could just make out a bunk to one side: there seemed to be someone lying on it. But there was no movement and he couldn't be sure it wasn't just a blanket roll or other gear.

Then something exploded in the back of his head and he was driven forward three faltering steps before his legs folded under him. He dropped to his knees, swaying, blindly reaching up to touch his throbbing head: his fingers encountered something wet and sticky.

Then the immediate scene wavered and dimmed and he had a sensation of falling. He stretched out on the packed earth floor, barely conscious. Turning his head painfully an inch or two he saw

Mustang kick the muddy rifle out of reach, noticed again the boot with the ankle-high uppers, laced firmly to encase Mustang's crippled foot. *No moccasins now.*

As he watched, unable to move, that boot lifted off the floor, swung back then forward, and crashed into his temple.

There were bursting lights shot through with streaking red for a few brief seconds, then only darkness.

*   *   *

He didn't know how much later he felt rough boot leather jabbing up and down his ribs, a hand shaking his shoulder painfully, so that his head jarred back and forth loosely on his neck. But each movement wrenched a groan from him and he rolled on to one side, moaning as his tried to open his eyes.

'C'mon! C'mon! Wake up, you swamp-rat bastard! You'll miss all the fun!'

Cade got his eyes open and squinted, seeing Mustang standing over him: even in that stance he favoured his left leg, keeping some of the weight off it, knee slack. A fist smashed into Cade's jaw, wrenching his head painfully to one side. Another crashed between his eyes, sent his vision exploding and spinning, dragging comet trails across come-and-go darkness. He shook his head instinctively in an effort to clear it and regretted it instantly.

Mustang laughed out loud as Cade's face twisted and contorted in agony. 'Hey! This is gonna be good, huh? Just you an' me — and my mangled foot!'

He kicked Cade in the ribs again and after he could drag down enough breath, Chris gestured to the bunk with his eyes: he could see there was a man lying there, now his sight had adjusted to the dimness.

'Why not make it a party? Invite him, too.'

Another jarring, painful blow to the face.

'He's had his party — or some of it.'
He chuckled again, the braided hair
tails shaking. 'Got a hangover now.
Have to give him some treatment when
he joins us again.'

'Is it Duggan?'

Mustang sobered. 'Shut up!' He
twisted fingers in Cade's hair, yanked
him to a sitting position and slammed
his head against the wall. Chris almost
passed out again — and discovered his
hands were tied behind him. He spat a
little blood and set a bleak stare on the
breed's ugly face.

'Rememberin' those badlands, huh?'

'Hell! I never forget 'em!' Mustang
held out his crippled foot in its special
boot. 'This makes sure I don't.'

'How'd it feel, crawling across that
alkali? Get a notion of what a hoss with
a broken leg might've had to put up
with? Didn't find any wagon of gold, I
guess.'

The breed stared back, face impas-
sive, then suddenly went into a kicking,
punching frenzy, leaving Chris bleeding

and less than semi-conscious when it was over. When he got his senses back, he saw it was dark outside. The fire still glowed in the cabin and Mustang had lit a storm lantern and hung it on a nail in the wall. The bunk was in shadow and there wasn't a sound from it. Chris strained, listening for breathing, but could detect nothing. If it was Duggan, there was a good chance he was dead after Mustang had finished with him. The rain had stopped. He didn't know if that was good or bad — nor did he care right now.

The wrangler was eating, and while chewing the food, glanced up and saw that Cade was coming round.

'Hungry?' he asked and flung the food scraps off the plate into the sheriff's face. The pieces of fat and half-chewed meat and a chop bone fell into his lap, with some beans and gravy. 'Guess I'll eat later,' he gritted.

'*And* you'll eat what I want you to! Worms, lizards, dog shit!' Mustang laughed, lurched up and Chris saw the near-empty whiskey bottle on the table that had been screened by the breed's body. He flung the tin plate at Cade who managed to get his head out of the way, but earned more callous blows. He sagged in the middle, his ribs bruised and mighty sore. Mustang stood over him, boots planted firmly now.

'Hope you're enjoyin' this, Cade. But it ain't even the beginnin'. I'm tired, wore myself out on that sonuver Duggan there. I'll get to you proper come mornin'. Might even let you see sunup. Likely to be your last.' Broken teeth flashed in a cold grin. 'Know what I mean?'

'You're too subtle for me, Mustang.'

A lip lifted in a sneer. 'You might be surprised how *subtle* I can get! Like skinnin' you alive, a little at a time. See? Do an arm or a shoulder, then when you're screamin' and bleedin', I might decide to have some grub or a shot of booze, take a nap — leave you there till you pass out. You'll never know just when I'm gonna start again. Hell, I could make you last a week — two!'

The sadistic talk was getting Mustang all excited and, breath hissing through the nostrils of his hooked nose, he reached for the whiskey bottle and tilted it against his lips. He took a long draught, blew out his cheeks and dropped into his chair again.

'Woooo! Gittin' a l'il bit drunky! Feels good, but be better I work on you sober. Can think better, do all the *subtle* stuff, make sure you feel pain every damn minute I let you . . . live!'

He came across and kicked and beat at Cade until the man was unconscious — and then did it some more. He was swaying when he finished, grabbed the bottle and drained it. Then he stood there swaying like a weed in a high wind, lifted one arm and groped his way to a bunk on the opposite wall. He was muttering as he crashed on to the tangled blankets.

He writhed and muttered unintelligible sounds, then was still and soon the snores began.

Cade, bleeding, throbbing, sat there against the wall struggling with his bonds. But it was no use: Mustang knew his knots and these were tight and cutting off the circulation in his hands and fingers. He looked around through aching eyes, the left one almost closed with swelling. There was the fire — maybe he could flick a coal on to the hearth and press the ropes against it . . .

In theory, it sounded a possibility, but all he did was burn his hands and he was afraid he would do major harm to his fingers as he couldn't feel them well enough to know whether they were being burned to the bone or not.

He slumped, looked at Mustang on the bunk. The man would really go to work on him in the morning, and it would be mighty painful — and prolonged. *One long day's dying* . . .

Then a voice said, 'Give him another ten minutes or so to fall into deep sleep. Then I'll get a knife and cut you free.'

Chris hurt his neck, he twisted it so fast and hard.

Duggan — if that's who it was — was half-sitting on the bunk, a dirty bandage on one hand, just a vague grey shape, his breathing hard and wet-sounding, mixed with an occasional moan.

'Jesus! I thought you were dead.'

'So — so did I. More importantly so did Mustang.' He gave a long moan. 'Not so sure I'm not . . . You're Cade, eh?'

'Yeah. An you're Duggan?'

'Mostly. Bits of me missing — ' He held up the hand with the bandage. 'Coupla fingertips gone, but mostly I'm Brick Duggan.' His words suddenly began to slur and trailed off.

Then he fell back on the bunk unconscious.

Chris Cade swore. Looked like he was going to be hogtied here until Mustang came round after all.

* * *

Despite himself and the throbbing pain of his bruised and battered body, he

141

slept for a time.

It was pitch black when he awoke and brought a hand up to press gently on his left side. *Man!* Mustang had bent his ribs well and truly —

Then he realized his hands were free.

He brought both up in front of his swollen, blood-streaked face, wriggled his fingers, could barely make them out. The fire had died all the way down and the storm lantern was low on oil. He flicked his eyes towards Duggan's bunk, barely able to see out of the left one, the flesh was so closed around it.

'Duggan?' he asked in a hoarse whisper at the same time hearing a grunting snore from the bunk Mustang had fallen on. 'You — with us . . . ?'

'Only just.'

Chris jerked his head around: Duggan had spoken from floor level, somewhere off to his left.

'Where the hell are you?'

'F-fell outta the bunk an' crawled to the shelf where he keeps his knives.' Duggan was breathless, his words slurred. 'W-was gonna stab the bastard, finish him. But I panicked, thought I mightn't do it . . . right the first time. So I cut your bonds — figured you could mebbe help if he jumped me. We can stab him together, huh?'

Chris was rubbing his wrists, fore-arms and hands briskly. His buttocks were numb, too, and it was a small touch of hell just to move, but —

'Gimme a coupla minutes. I'll help . . . How bad are you?'

'A tunnel fell in on me once, busted me up all to hell. I'm feelin' not quite as good as I felt then.'

Cade couldn't help grinning: Duggan couldn't be too bad if he could joke like that. He edged across the floor.

'Two of us together might make one man right now. Mebbe we better just hightail it — or at least find a gun.'

'Your six-gun's somewhere here, and the rifle — think he kicked it under a bunk or a cupboard.'

'Judas!' Chris exclaimed remember-ing. 'He's got a sawn-off somewhere!

143

Hate to have him cut loose with that in here!'

There was a brief silence, except for Duggan's ragged breathing. 'You got a point. Rain's stopped. Might be a nice night outside. We go look? Take a walk, mebbe . . . ?'

Cade hesitated: he needed a weapon, preferably one of his own guns. Mustang was stirring now on his bunk as the alcohol wore off and no doubt the sound of their voices, even though only ragged whispers, was penetrating his sleep fog . . .

'We better get out,' Cade decided, grunted as he got to his knees and reached out to help Duggan. He felt the knife the man had used on the ropes: it seemed to be some kind of kitchen utensil, small-bladed, no weight in the handle. Useless for throwing, and if he had to get close enough to use it by hand, well, it would be too close with a maniac like McLeary, and Chris in his present condition.

Still, he kept hold of it as, on all

fours, they made for the door. They were within reach of it and Chris felt for the latch, only to find it was padlocked — *and the chain rattled . . .*

'The hell . . . '

It was the startled, slurred reaction of Mustang coming out of his sleep. In a flash, used to living on his wits and meeting any dangerous situation pronto, Mustang swore, recognizing the clank of the chain and padlock, and rolled out of the bunk on to the floor.

Through the dense dark, Chris went cold as he heard the hammers of the sawn-off shotgun cock. 'Goin' somewhere, Cade?' A brief laugh. 'Yeah, you sure are: straight *to hell!*'

Chris flung himself at Duggan, flattening the man against the floor as the shotgun blasted. The muzzle flash was brilliant and the thunder deafening. The charge hit the door, splintered planks and rattled it madly against the chain.

And, in that instant of flash, Chris saw the muddy butt of his rifle poking out from beneath a cupboard, not five feet away. He rolled over the moaning Duggan, launched himself bodily as the second barrel of the shotgun roared, some of the buckshot sending clods of the earthen floor pattering and bursting against the sagging front door.

Chris's fingers touched the rifle butt, feeling most of the mud had dried. He rolled on to his back, hearing Mustang fling the empty shotgun aside and a scrabbling sound that could only be the killer trying to free his six-gun from where his rig hung above the bunk.

Chris reared up on to his knees, rifle butt braced into his hip, working lever and trigger, hoping the rain and mud hadn't jammed the action. The first shot was a misfire and he had to jerk hard to eject the complete cartridge out of the port. Mustang had his gun now and triggered as he flung himself off the bunk. The rifle barrel swung to where the gunflash was and four fast thundering shots filled the cabin deafeningly, powder-smoke thick and choking, mixing with that left by the shotgun's blasts.

There was a clatter, a gritted curse. Through the dim fog, Chris sensed rather than saw Mustang lurching towards him, six-gun wavering, determined to kill his tormentor before he cashed in his own chips . . .

But he was already dead on his feet, his chest torn apart by Cade's bullets. He began to sag. The Colt fired and jumped from his fast-weakening grasp. He dropped to his knees, reaching out a clawed hand towards the kneeling sheriff.

Well short of target, he fell, and died noisily, thrashing in a welter of his own blood.

9

No One Gets Out Alive

Early sunlight slanting through the ragged hole Mustang had shot in the front door, blowing it half off its leather hinges, woke Chris Cade.

He was lying on the floor, a couple of feet from the body of Mustang, who was sprawled in a dark oval with uneven edges — a big pool of his own blood which had partly soaked into the packed-earth floor. Mustang's mouth was drawn back in a snarl, his last gesture at a life that had allowed him to inflict pain, practice sadism and debauchery for far too long. Well, it had ended for him now, painfully, with perhaps just a taste of the kind of agony he had put his countless victims through.

Cade was stiff and sore, mouth dry,

148

head throbbing. His left eye was blurred. He looked across to Duggan. The man was either sleeping or unconscious — either way he was still breathing and that was good.

At least he was still alive.

Straining and grunting, Chris got Duggan up on to the bunk properly. The man groaned and opened his eyes. He was a big man, solid muscles, wide shoulders and a thick chest. The grimy bandage had slipped off his calloused left hand and Cade grimaced when he saw the mangled fingers: congealed blood where the first joint of each digit should have been.

He got some water from an iron pot, and a rag, lifted the hand and bathed away some of the filth. He saw traces of pus there on all four fingers and by then Duggan was conscious enough to snatch his hand away. He held it up, staring at its mutilation.

'Bastard did 'em one at a time — with a blunt chisel.'

'That'd be Mustang. World has to be

a slightly better place with him gone from it. At least he chose your left hand — unless you're a southpaw?'

Duggan tried a smile but it was strained. 'No, I'm right handed. He wanted that unharmed so I could write out my statement and sign it properly.' Cade looked puzzled and Duggan said, ' 'Report' might be better — a summary of the results of my investigations . . . as long as I made 'em comply with the desires of Judge Kirk and friends.' He saw more puzzlement on Cade's battered, misshapen face and added, 'I'm a surveyor-engineer and I've been checking out a section of country for the judge and his associates.'

'Magruder included?'

'I understand he's a partner with Kirk in Padlock.'

Chris found an old flour sack, rinsed it and tore it into strips. He bound Duggan's fingers as well as he could, padding the tender ends, Duggan gritting his teeth and biting back epithets as Cade worked. 'That ought to help. Where else did the sonuver get to you?'

'He was starting on my toe. Think I lost the big one off my right foot, and the little one off my left. Feels kinda strange, anyway.'

Chris removed the man's big, lace-up half-boots and found the wounds just as Duggan had described. Working with water and more strips of the flour sack, Cade said,

'What were you surveying?'

'The judge swore me to secrecy — Bible and all, very solemn — and I gave my word.' He smiled crookedly at the look Cade gave him. 'It's gone by the board now, of course. You know anything about terrain in general? The way the land lies, stratum, curvature and oblique angles, pressures of water that flows through or across diatomaceous earth in the form of rivers and creeks?' He held up a hand as Cade kept shaking his head and started to speak. 'Rhetorical question, Cade. Of course you don't, unless you, too, are a surveyor and know something of hydrography. No? Well, in a nutshell, the Arkansas River that traverses this part of Kansas meanders like a drunken cowpoke on payday; myriad creeks and small tributaries branch out through low hills that leave depressions between. Can you picture what I mean?'

'Clear enough — gulches or arroyos between low hills. It's pretty much the same anywhere you ride — Texas, New Mexico, Louisiana — though it might be a mite greener there with their bayous.'

'You have the general idea.' Duggan paused, working out what he was about to say. 'Those depressions — what you call gulches and arroyos — many were old water-courses. Oh, hundreds, thousands of years ago, maybe, but they're indications of how and where the rivers flowed at that time.'

Chris waited, an idea forming.

'If some of those low hills or the raised land were removed, by blasting or hydro-jet, a man could change the course of any present-day river, turn what are now middling-sized creeks into deepwater, fast flowing streams; take things a step further, and selectively remove your hills, and you could even make a lake — big, small, perhaps something worthy of being called an inland sea — fed by those diverted rivers. The scale depends on your bank balance.'

He let the words hang and Cade stared at him fixedly for a long minute, then nodded slowly.

'Vaguely recollect seeing a folder on the judge's desk marked *RIVER-SLAKE* with smaller print in brackets 'Formerly Reno Creek'. Anything to do with your survey?'

'Yes, the judge has formed his own consortium to turn Reno Creek, now a small, mostly no-account town straddling the cattle trails to Dodge, into a much larger, and prosperous town, serviced by riverboats, passenger, cattle, or freight-carrying vessels. And it's quite feasible.'

'But . . . ?'

'Always that little word, isn't there . . . ? The way the judge wants to do it would mean flooding all of the presently thriving ranches and farms in the basin, submerging them forever under many feet of water.'

He paused again, strain showing now as the injuries from his ordeal began to catch up with him.

'I'll make some coffee and see what grub's available. We'll eat and talk some more after.'

Duggan nodded, glancing towards Mustang's body.

'I can get him outside first if you like,' Chris offered, but Duggan swallowed and shook his head, while Cade, who felt as if he had survived a stampede of buffalo running over him, cooked eggs and sowbelly and beans. When Duggan was on his second cup of coffee, he said:

'The problem was, the judge and his friends didn't want to hear my alternative to what they had in mind.'

Cade looked around sharply. 'They wanted to flood the ranches and farmland?'

Duggan nodded.

'I s'ppose I shouldn't be surprised. I've met the judge and he seems mighty avaricious to me. But why would he want to ruin all those settlers if you have a good alternative?'

'I picked up from what some of his men said that the land they homesteaded was once open range and used more or less permanently by Magruder, one of Kirk's partners.'

'So the homestead law beat him and this way of ruining them is too good for Magruder and Kirk to pass up. *Do* you have an alternative?'

'I do, but it means some tunnelling, which is more expensive and time-consuming, and some blasting of convergent channels. The judge and his friends have their minds set on their own ideas for a man-made lake. My way, they'd have a wide, fast-flowing deep-water river, that would pass the town by half a mile, which is an ideal distance for building a riverboat landing outside of town. But they want the lake.'

'Quicker — and cheaper. And a chance to settle old scores.'

'Yeah, when we couldn't agree I stuck by my findings, the best and safest way: in fact, the only way that stood a chance of Washington's approval. They didn't want me to send in that report, because it would give the government agency I'm responsible to, a choice, so they had a problem and, also, if I was to come to any harm or have a suspicious 'accident', there'd be hell to pay and an investigation that would turn this land on its ear. So the judge and his friends arranged a different kind of 'accident' for me.'

Chris suddenly saw it. 'You were meant to be trampled by that stallion, not Mel Hawkins!'

'Yeah, but Mel made the mistake of trying to grab the bridle to save me, and the horse turned on him.'

'Well, I'll be damned! All in front of dozens of witnesses. Just one of those things — a knucklehead bronc going berserk because some idiot dropped a firework under its belly. Nothing suspicious ... Unless you knew Mustang McLeary had trained the horse! And Casey set off the firecracker.'

'That's it. They whisked me back to Padlock pronto. I'd picked up a few bangs and bruises from being thrown out of the saddle, but nothing too serious. They spread the word that I'd quit and next thing I know, I'm being held prisoner up here — with *that*!'

Duggan gestured savagely towards the body near the sagging front door.

'He was supposed to make you change your mind about the report? Approve the judge's and Magruder's plans to flood the basin without mentioning the spreads already there?'

Duggan nodded, face tight and pale. 'Just as well you showed — I couldn't've held out much longer. But, you're a lawman: you can take my deposition and get it to my agency, can't you?'

'Trouble is, I'm not a real lawman. I've never been sworn in. I signed a contract — for a cut-price wage — under duress. With that kind of background, I'm not sure your deposition'd be worth the paper it was written on.'

'Well, I do have a certain amount of . . . integrity!' Duggan said kind of stiffly. 'I've worked damned hard to get it over the years!'

'Sure, that'd count, but a sharp lawyer would soon tear that deposition to ribbons. My background's not as pure as yours and if I was the only witness to your statement . . . '

He spread his hands, letting it ride.

Duggan looked alarmed. 'Then, I have to get out of here! Does Magruder know you were coming up to this linecamp?'

'Yeah. Deliberately gave me wrong directions so I'd ride into a couple of ambushes he'd set up.'

Duggan's gaze sharpened. 'You're here. So you must've dodged the ambushers.'

'We traded some lead, but I did get past 'em.'

'Man! That's no mean feat. Not that it helps much, right now, I suppose.'

'There's a US marshal stationed at Kinlaw, the county seat. He'd take your deposition and it'd stand up in any court in the land, but it's a fair ride and — '

Duggan snorted. 'Hell, I can make it!'

Cade shrugged with a crooked smile. 'Mebbe, but it'll be tough goin'. In any case, we better get outta here. Once Magruder finds out his ambushes didn't work, he'll send Montana or someone to check this place.'

★ ★ ★

They moved fast, but not quite fast enough.

Montana led in a close-riding bunch of four armed men as Cade and Duggan cleared the linecamp and headed across the face of the slope.

Chris spotted them high above, just coming out of the trees on the south side of the linecabin. He jerked a hand at Duggan who seemed to be suffering a good deal of pain in the jolting saddle, kept sliding his feet out of the stirrups to take the weight off them. He was also upset at having to leave most of his surveying gear he had stowed in the cabin, though he brought the theodolite's scope.

'They belong to me, my own personal tools!' he objected. 'Cost thousands! I'll never be able to replace 'em.'

'If you live through this maybe your company'll give you a new set for getting that survey report through.'

Duggan grunted, and fumblingly unscrewed the sighting scope with its brass scale from the section of the theodolite he had brought with him. He thrust the scope into his saddle-bag, discarded the rest and lifted the reins, ready to ride about ten seconds before Chris spotted Montana's bunch.

'Well, we've wasted time but now you'll be able to see their faces while they're shooting at us!' growled Cade, spurring away, Duggan racing his dapple-rumped grey along-side, looking happier now.

'I'll tell you which one is aiming at you!'

Cade snorted. 'Save your breath and hit that slope yonder. We're goin' over and down.'

'My God! It's . . . almost vertical!'

'Yeah, mighty dangerous. Might make the others look for a safer way down; it'll take 'em a lot longer to find it. Give us time to get away.'

Then they were at the edge of the steep drop and Cade deliberately rammed his smoke into Duggan's grey which the man had hauled up. He was half-standing in the stirrups looking down at the hazardous drop.

'I don't think we — '

That was as far as he got when Cade's smoke hit the grey's rump and nudged it over the edge. Duggan gave a wild yell, holding the reins tightly, unable to get a firm grip because of his mutilated hand. But Cade was right alongside and felt his belly bounce with the sudden drop. The smoke snorted but had enough sense not to waste time turning its head either way; just looked down and ahead, choosing the best path, trying to control its slide.

Not that they were given much choice: the only way was down, and much too steep for either man's liking. Only truly desperate fugitives would have risked this.

Well, if Duggan didn't realize just how desperate the situation was, he surely was about to find out . . .

He lurched forward on to the horse's arched neck, banging his mouth hard and tasting blood. He tried to rear up straighter but the gravity forces were too strong, held him pinned in an awkward position, giving him a perfect view of a gravelly slope with a field of keg-sized boulders beyond.

No patches of thick brush to break any fall. Just plenty of hard ground to break bones.

Then something buzzed over their heads — *several* somethings: bullets.

On the rim, Montana and his crew were shooting down the steep drop, but it was so vertical that they grew dizzy leaning far out so as to find their fleeing targets.

Every shot missed.

The fugitives were almost standing in the stirrups now, bodies thrown back on to their horses' rumps, reins stretched to the limit. The mounts had raised a cloud of choking dust, the skidding hoofs of the stiff-legged, rump-down animals tearing away the inches of wet top soil from the rain, gouging up the dry earth underneath.

The cloud obscured them and Montana yelled to hold their fire and start looking for another way down . . .

163

By the time the fugitives reached the bottom of the drop — both somewhat startled to find they were still alive — Cade and Duggan were choking in the dust. The animals were panting, foam flying from their bit-cramped mouths, eyes rolling.

But they were quick to recover when they felt the ground levelling beneath their aching legs.

Duggan wiped his right hand down his face, leaving finger tracks through the dirt.

'I hope the rest . . . of the trail . . . is better,' he gasped.

'A breeze,' Chris assured him, having no idea what the trail was like. 'Keep going. They'll find a way down and be on our tails before long.'

'You're not the most optimistic man I would've chosen for a companion, Cade, if I'd had a choice.'

'And there's the rub, eh? You're stuck with me, so quit bitchin' and let's move before we have to try to outrun a whole slew of bullets.'

'See? That's what I call 'pessimism'! Even if you're probably right. And it's catching, damnit! I'm beginning to think we probably won't make it out of here, anyway.'

Chris smiled wryly.

'Don't worry about it: that's life — no one gets out alive.'

10

Big Deal

Crowe sauntered into the judge's office and ran into a tirade of curses from Kirk, finishing the bitter denunciation with, 'Where the hell've you been? It's an hour since I sent for you!'

Crowe looked at the anger darkening Kirk's face and arched his scarred eyebrows, hitting his forehead hard with the heel of one hand. 'Aw gee, is it?' he asked dolefully, without any touch of sincerity. Then when he figured the judge was within a hair of apoplexy, he shrugged. 'I was . . . er . . . out of town and only got your message about ten minutes ago.'

'Still running the risk of jealous husbands, are you? Well, you're a damn fool, but that's your concern. Being where I want you, when I want you is mine!'

Crowe, unperturbed, dropped into his usual chair. 'What's the big deal, Judge?'

Kirk's eyes narrowed almost to slits and he made obvious and difficult efforts to get himself under control. When he spoke his voice was milder but there was an edge of steel audible. ''Big deal' is right! That damn Cade's a lot harder to kill than anyone expected! Magruder gave him wrong directions that'd steer him into several ambushes and he damn well shot his way past them all!'

Crowe arched his eyebrows again 'Warned you right from the start you'd never control him like you wanted to.'

'I'm not interested in hindsight!' A big fist slammed down on to the desk. Crowe didn't seem bothered by it. 'Magruder's sent word that Cade has killed Mustang at the linecamp and is on the run with Duggan in the sierras. Pat's sent Montana after them with some men but I want you up there! You make sure neither of them get away. I want them both dead.'

Crowe at last showed some real interest. 'If Duggan turns up with bullets in him, we'll have more US marshals in here than fleas on a coon-dog.'

'That's something we'll worry about after! The main thing now is to stop them. Dead!'

Crowe looked doubtful. 'Judge, I don't think it's a good idea to bushwhack Duggan. Whatever happens to him has to look like a natural accident, or we're gonna — '

'If his body's never found it won't matter will it?'

The big man nodded slowly. '*If* . . . '

Kirk's eyes glinted. 'I believe I can claim to be pretty adept at hiding things when I put my mind to it.'

Crowe took a minute to think about that, then nodded curtly, stood without hurry. 'Well, if you say so — 'til now, leastways.'

'Take whatever and whoever you need.'

'I work better alone.'

'As long as you get the job done — satisfactorily . . . Remember, I only pay for results!'

The door closed quietly and outside, Crowe said quietly to himself,

'You'll pay anyway, Judge. I don't take this job lightly, goin' after a government man; not to mention findin' myself up agin someone like Chris Cade.'

★   ★   ★

The relentless pursuit went on all day.

Chris thought at least two more men had joined Montana but couldn't be sure because of the heat waves dancing between him and the hill he was glassing.

He knew this country reasonably well, but only from what he remembered when he had been through here with Boss Fredericks's trail herds. They had to get off the well-used trails and once they turned into the hills proper, would have to keep searching for accessible high country so he could locate landmarks he recalled.

Duggan had traipsed through much of the country on his search for the best terrain for changing the course of the river and its tributaries. He admitted it would be comparatively easy to drain them into the basin and in time it would make a decent sized lake, but he couldn't bring himself to recommend it when he knew there were hard-working folk going to lose all they had built up over the years once the basin was flooded — just because of some grudge-bearing cattleman who already had more land than he would ever use.

And he had resented the judge and his cronies thinking that they could buy him off, as an answer to their problems. *'Come in, Brick, sit down. Just a few words . . . '*

It wasn't so much a direct bribe — not in so many words. But at a sign from Judge Kirk, Burl, who was in the office for the meeting, along with Pat

Magruder, picked up a satchel he was carrying and took out a cloth-wrapped bundle. Watching Duggan's puzzled face, he set it on the table, unwrapped it and revealed a short bar of gold. It was about nine inches long, an inch across the widest part and three-quarters of an inch thick. Obviously, it had been rough-cast in a sand box, but was unmistakably gold. Duggan didn't touch it, ran his hard gaze around the councillors.

'Where did that come from?'

'You don't need to know — only that there's a lot more of it. You could find some heading your way,' the judge said slowly, watching Duggan for his reaction mighty closely.

'I . . . don't think so, Judge, and I know I couldn't influence my bosses in any way, no matter how much gold you offered.'

His refusal had almost cost him his life, had sure as hell cost him plenty of pain and *that* wasn't over by a long shot! But he was a man who placed a great store in a man's integrity. And he was prepared to stand up for what he believed in . . .

'*Did* you find anything unusual on your survey?' Chris asked, jarring Duggan's thoughts back to the present. 'You know, somethin' the judge mightn't want found or even known about . . . ?'

'Not sure what you mean, but no. Only thing that puzzled me was half a hill had been blasted down into an arroyo for no good reason that I could see. Not too long ago.'

'Blasted? Couldn't've been a natural land-slip after heavy rain? Often happens, you know.'

'Sure, but I use a lot of dynamite in my work; I know the signs — this had been blasted. Must've been a good-sized 'bang', too. Could've been Magruder trying his hand at changing the course of that part of the river, for his ranch, though a little too far away to be effective, I'd've thought. Could've been a whole house buried under that dirt for all I could tell.'

They were in a fold of the hills now and Cade gestured to a steep rise, indicating that they should go that way and find a vantage point from which to see the backtrail.

It was a hot, zigzagging climb and they were sweating and the horses were blowing hard when they came to a boulder pile that offered shade as well as a view of the country they wanted to check.

Duggan used the magnifying sight-glass from his theodolite while Chris shaded his eyes, but had trouble making out details. Duggan handed him the glass, shielding its bright brass with one hand in case it flashed in the sun. He pointed north-east.

'Brush is moving over there. I think I saw a man's hat — I'm sure it's them.'

So was Cade after a long study, changing focus, sweeping the brush thicket very slowly. 'Yeah! Looks like five or six riders.' He glanced at the afternoon sky. 'They're not gonna give up.'

'They'll have to soon. Be sundown in a little over an hour.'

'I reckon they're gonna keep coming after dark.'

Duggan swore softly. 'Cold tack tonight, again, then.'

'It's more serious than that, Brick. I've been thinking and I can't see that they'd risk a couple of murders just to stop you from putting in your report on the chance it'll be acccepted in preference to the lake idea.'

'Well, flooding that basin is tanta-mount to murder. I mean they know folk are there, but they still aim to do it . . . *want* to do it.'

'Mmmmm, mebbe. You've had more experience with government than me — thank God! — but why d'you figure they'll favour your idea when, like you said, it'll cost more and take more time?'

Duggan smiled, his face drawn with his aches and pains. 'As you say, I've had a lot of dealings with government, specially the money men who have to foot the bills for our engineering projects *and* be able to justify them to Congress. See, what I didn't say earlier was that for some time now the department has had a notion about diverting some of the rivers in this territory, to open up the country for settlement faster.'

'Well, don't get too damn technical — I ain't all that educated, you know.'

'It's straight enough. Any ruling government wants to stay that way: *ruling*. Having a good record of public works almost guarantees they'll get Congress's vote. Folk want better transport than just wagons prone to Indian attack and bad weather. Railroads are fine, but there's still so much land available, most well past the current heads-of-track. Rivers can offer speed as well as comfort, you put the right kind of boats on 'em . . . and you don't have to lay hundreds of miles of iron track, either.'

'So your department would be mighty interested in your recommendations, even if they don't seem to gel with what Judge Kirk's group want.'

'Right. For return of money and time invested, a placid lake, while picturesque and useful in many ways, won't stand up against a deepwater river with boats: rivers can carry men hundreds, thousands of miles; they can stop and go ashore wherever they see land they like and settle it; eventually, new railheads can link up with riverboat landings and so on. A navigable river has a big advantage over a lake.'

'For opening up the country, you mean. Yeah, I can see that.' There was a trace of bitterness in Cade's words and Duggan looked at him sharply. 'But, guess I'm kinda selfish — I like the wide open spaces with not too many people. I like to ford rivers without having to dodge a slew of riverboats. I like to hear the kinda lonesome whistle of a locomotive way out on the prairie with a herd of buffalo scattered round, grazing, or a lone wolf watching on a rise, and know there won't be another train for a week or more.'

Duggan laughed shortly. 'You're a loner born and bred, Chris, that's your trouble.'

Cade admitted it, but he also admitted that he was aware it was a losing battle: 'Civilization' in all its forms was bound to catch up with him sooner or later.

'I guess I'll adapt, but I've still got a hunch that there's more to this than just risking some government department accepting your idea over the judge's.'

Duggan shook his head. 'There's no other reason why the judge and his men are after me — I'm sure of that.'

'There's gotta be something else, Brick. Something they don't want endangered by your survey.'

'Well, what the hell could it be?' Duggan spoke impatiently. 'It's either have a pretty lake which would probably bring in some extra folk and let the town expand a little, or a swift-flowing river that'll certain-sure bring a lot of new trade, not just passengers, but there'll be logging rafts from upstream, cattle-and-freight boats, and maybe other advantages I haven't thought about. The extra water passing through that land would probably make it more fertile, too, in the long run.'

'So would a lake, wouldn't it?'

'Ye-es, but I doubt it would improve or equal the area of land being drowned by its formation.'

'OK, you keep sayin' 'fast-flowin' ' rivers . . . '

'A sluggish river's not much good for anything. It's simple enough to make sure there's a good flow when you know how — just a matter of adjusting the gradient narrowing or expanding the banks, ironing out curves. It takes time, but just accept that it can be done, Chris, and it's far more advantageous in the long run.'

Chris looked thoughtful now. 'If it's got a good, strong, steady current, would it gouge out a deeper water course — in time?'

'Sure, all rivers do, but that's all to the good, and we'd allow for that. All this is possible, Chris, but that's not what the judge or his friends would be concerned with.'

Chris lifted a cautionary finger. 'Now, mebbe you're wrong about that! Mebbe that's exactly what's got the judge's underwear in a knot.'

Duggan frowned. 'What the hell're you talking about?'

Chris lifted the glass and ran it over the far mountain where they had seen the movement in the thicket.

'We better find ourselves somewhere to hole-up for the night; somewhere we can defend easily and get away from pronto if we have to.'

That kind of talk made Duggan uneasy and he took the glass and put it in his saddle-bags. 'I'm all for that! But I still don't know what you're thinking.'

Chris smiled crookedly. 'Not sure myself, but I might have it worked out a little more by the time we find a place for tonight. Let's go!'

★   ★   ★

They located a place on a ledge high up a steep slope that would be easy to defend — and still left an escape route at one end, shielded from below by a ragged row of boulders.

They took it in turns to stand guard and during his stint, getting on towards morning, Chris shook Duggan by the shoulder. The big engineer came awake with a rush, grunting in pain as he grabbed his rifle with his injured hands.

'God-*damn*! What the hell time is it?'

'Coupla hours to sunup. Listen, you said they tried to bribe you, right? With gold?'

Duggan groaned. 'Christ! Couldn't this wait?'

'Was — it — gold?' Chris insisted.

Duggan nodded curtly. 'Yeah, an *ingot*, just a rough sandcasting, nothing like the banks or army use.'

'I think I know why they don't want your river.'

Duggan curtailed his irritation, looked around. 'All right, but what about us right now? Is it still safe here?'

'Yeah, when I came down, it was all clear. This'll just take a couple minutes, then I'll go back, and you can think about my theory . . . '

Duggan was plainly nervous: having six armed men after you with the sole intention of killing you was not a recipe for steady nerves . . . or easy sleep.

But Cade was true to his word: he was brief and gave Duggan plenty of food for serious thought.

'Two years ago an army pay wagon was held up in Trident Pass about twenty miles downtrail. There were seven soldiers riding with it and it's thought they were all massacred. *Thought* because their bodies were never found — only a lot of blood — too much blood, and many cartridge cases. The wagon was driven away, presumably with the dead troopers and disappeared. The best explanation is that it might've hit one of those sandholes, which you'd know about.'

'Where the crust is only inches thick and underneath is a loose, almost mobile sand?'

'That's it. They can be big or small, can't they?'

Duggan was dubious. 'Ye-ah, but I don't know of any big enough to swallow a whole wagon, and I guess the team as well as the soldiers — '

'No, not likely, but possible.' Chris paused, tried to see Duggan's face but it was still too dark. 'Or, it could have been buried in one of the hundreds of arroyos. Drive it in, use dynamite to blow down a few tons of rock and earth — ' He gestured with his hands. 'Gone from sight.'

Duggan moved slowly, hipping around on his bedroll, straining, too, to see Cade's face.

'The arroyo I found with half a hillside blasted down into it?' Duggan was tensed now, alert with this new thought.

'Possible?'

Duggan was quiet for a time and Chris's ears were straining to hear any unnatural sounds like clothing scraping against rock or brush, the clink of a hoof, or dull ringing of a gun barrel clipping a protruding boulder . . .

'I'd have to check my survey figures to be sure but that arroyo I found, would most likely be an ideal channel for one of the rivers I've recommended for redirection, and if it flowed through and uncovered . . . ? *My God!*'

Their gazes met even if they couldn't see each other's eyes. Chris asked tightly,

'That sound like a good enough reason to make sure your figures are never accepted . . . ? Or even considered?'

Before Duggan could answer, the night exploded with gunfire on the high ground above the ledge *and* the slope on the same level as their ledge on their right.

11

Death Trail South

'They're afoot!'

Even as he dived for the ground, twisting so as to turn the rifle towards the ragged line of flashes above, Cade yelled to Duggan who was finding his own boulder for shelter. 'They couldn't get horses up that steep slide, so they must've climbed up on foot.'

'The sonuvers are there however they got there!' Duggan panted, holding his rifle awkwardly, with his mangled left hand unable to close firmly around the fore-end. But he got off three ragged shots before he had to huddle close to the rock while lead whined and screamed off it from above *and below* . . . to the right where Cade figured the men were on foot.

Cade sighted and fired, aware of the

fast-paling sky now. But the attackers would be the ones silhouetted against it. The ledge was still in the shadow of the mountain. He had the satisfaction of seeing a rifle come tumbling over the ridge up there and a man's upper body slumping far enough forward so that one arm dangled, and was still.

He ducked, thumbing fresh shells into the loading gate to replace the ones he had fired. Lead raked his shelter. He glanced at Duggan who was fumbling to reload, hampered by his mutilated fingers, thanks to Mustang.

'Brick!' Cade called in a low voice. 'Those men below are on foot. You can bet they left their horses a fair way off. That's our way out.'

Duggan tensed. 'What about the ones above?'

'Yeah, they could've rode up from the far side, likely did, it ain't so steep there, but they can't get their mounts all the way up, as high as they're shooting from.' He ducked down as a raging volley raked the ledge — he figured they must have all emptied their rifles there were so many shots. When the shooting stopped and echoes were rolling away through the coming dawn, he called again to Duggan.

'We can be outta here and down past those below before the ones up top can do anything, and this ledge'll jut out far enough to give us cover from the fire above. It's the only way, Brick . . . You game, *amigo*?'

'If it's the only way, I am.'

'Right. Give 'em a blast, rake the top, I'll get the horses and you be ready to hit leather pronto. You be all right making a run to the hoss?'

'I'll get there!'

Chris saw movement up top while Duggan answered, threw his rifle up and fired twice. A man grunted and there was a clatter: he'd taken a hit of some kind.

'OK!' Duggan called. 'Whenever you say!'

'Make 'em keep their heads down!'

Cade, crouching, ran behind the

boulders to where they had left the horses saddled. They would have to abandon their bedrolls and grubsacks, but hunger was better than eating hot lead.

He skidded and the mounts squealed, startled, no doubt on edge from all the shooting. Rifles were blasting from both directions and Duggan answered, Chris noticing how slow his shooting was because of his handicap.

Then he ripped the reins from under the big rocks they had used to ground-hitch the mounts, and swung up into the smoke's saddle. He paused long enough to thumb three cartridges into the rifle, filling it to capacity, tugged on the reins of Duggan's dappled grey and jammed home his spurs.

The smoke leaped forward, Duggan's grey following with a snort. Chris stretched out along his horse, wheeled in behind the biggest line of rocks, heard a distant yell from above as he was spotted. He cringed as the lead began flying, kicking dust almost from under the smoke's pounding hoofs, hornet-buzzing off higher rocks. Duggan was waiting, one leg bent to take the weight off his damaged foot, half-crouched, rifle held awkwardly.

Chris slowed, felt his hat jerk, but it stayed on his head as a bullet ventilated the crown. Duggan leapt for his grey, lost his rifle as he fumbled for the saddle horn.

'*Leave it!*' yelled Chris and slowed still more, ducking lower as lead whined overhead. Glancing beneath the arched, sweating neck of the smoke, he saw a man just below the rim they were riding for stand quickly, from behind a rock, lifting a rifle to his shoulder.

Chris fired his Winchester one-handed and the mount whinnied and shied. But his bullet struck the man, knocking him sprawling. He slid on his belly reaching for his dropped rifle, so it hadn't been a fatal hit. But the distraction had been long enough for Duggan to settle in leather and grab the reins from Cade. They leapt their mounts over the edge on to the steep, twisting ground, studded with loose shale, some hardy brush, deadfalls and uprooted stumps.

No wonder the bushwhackers hadn't been able to ride up; but now, Chris and Duggan had to *ride down*!

Fortunately it was easier going down: the sharp-eyed mounts could pick their trail and the men let them have their heads, crouching low, shooting, Duggan using his six-gun, when they saw signs of men.

Taken by surprise the killers hadn't been prepared for charging horses and one man fell screaming and kicking under Duggan's grey, almost unseating the engineer, but he managed to stay put. Chris, heart in mouth, lifted the smoke over the thrashing man and jarred heavily in the saddle, being thrown forward so that his face hit the smoke's hard skull. He saw stars but gripped tightly with knees and reins.

Men were yelling above, just the

occasional shot coming now. He risked a look over his shoulder and recognized Montana standing up, bawling at his men to bring up their horses, waving the others back into the fray: the men on foot had scattered when Chris and Duggan charged through.

They were clear now but the slope was deadly and required all their attention, weaving, reining back, wrenching this way, then that, lifting over a deadfall, hauling on the bit, legs stiff in the stirrups, then kicking in with the spurs to get the mounts to speed again.

Suddenly, they were through, on to a more manageable slope, and were able to slow to a less dangerous pace. But that also made them better targets for Montana's men. All they could do was zigzag and drop over risky rises on to the trail below, cutting corners. The bullets were close but they got down into the shadowed fold between the hills where the sun hadn't reached yet.

It was by no means dark enough to hide them, but the men on the slopes with the rising sun in their eyes would have difficulty finding their targets.

They rode on, shots cracking behind them but getting fainter: they knew then they were outdistancing the shooters.

But by that time, Montana and his mounted men had come down from the far side of the slope and were thundering around to where the men who had been afoot were running to the place they had tethered their mounts. The ramrod roared at them to hurry as he raced by, followed by two others.

By Cade's count, they still had four fully active killers after them . . .

The fugitives kept riding and it soon became obvious that their mounts were tiring, feeling all the effort they had put into breaking away down that steep mountain.

'We're losin' ground!' Chris yelled.

Before Duggan could answer there was a series of rifle shots and Cade's eyes widened as one of Montana's men threw up his arms and tumbled out of the saddle. Chris wrenched his head around, couldn't see where the shots had come from.

'You see that?' Duggan asked and in the instant they locked gazes there was another shot and a horse went down back there throwing the rider. 'What the hell . . . ?'

'Don't ask! Just keep ridin'!'

Chris was as puzzled as the engineer and heard several more shots. Two more mounts went down and when one of the unhorsed men staggered up groggily, another shot cracked and the man spun as if jerked by a rope and sprawled face down in a thrashing heap.

Someone was giving them covering fire!

He had no idea who it could be, nor did he care right now. *Just keep it up, feller, and I'll gladly give you a big hug later! Might even kiss you!*

Then the next rise of land blotted out the pursuit and Duggan started to haul rein.

'Keep going!' shouted Chris.

'But — whoever that is might need some help.'

Chris laughed shortly. 'Hey, we're the ones need help and he's givin' it to us. We'll thank him later, whoever he is! Now ride and don't let his efforts go to waste!'

So they raced on — and on — and on . . .

They watched the back trail but no rider showed. Whoever had helped them didn't seem to be in any hurry to meet up with them . . .

Back out of view of the fugitives, Montana found he was the only one still in the saddle. Two of his men lay dead, another with a leg wound, the pain from which was making him swear in a continuous stream.

Montana sat there and looked at the rider walking his horse out from a boulderfield down-slope, rifle held ready to shoot across his thighs.

The ramrod stiffened as he recognized him.

'What . . . what the *hell* you think

you're doing, Crowe!'

Crowe smiled thinly. 'Just helpin' out.'

'Kinda got your goddamn targets mixed, didn't you?'

Crowe shook his head slowly. 'Nope. Dunno if I ever told you, Montana, but I never did like you.'

Then the rifle whipped to his shoulder and Crowe shot Montana squarely through the heart.

*   *   *

Kinlaw was twice as big as Reno Creek.

The main street was graded, and regularly, by the looks of the flat surface which was free of stones that might get under a horse's shoes. Gutters were clear of rubbish and reasonably dry. The side streets were all signposted and the storefronts were neat, the paint clean if not fresh.

Folk were better dressed than those in the trail towns and moved at a more leisurely pace along the walks, which

194

seemed to be without ruts or grit. There were more brick or stone buildings, too, and two more churches by Cade's count. *This was a real progressive frontier town* . . .

He and Duggan were ragged, trail-stained to the point of looking like a couple of saddletramps, and sat their mounts on a small rise on the edge of town.

'If the marshal's as dapper as the town looks, we ought to get a square deal,' Duggan opined.

Cade nodded, but said cautiously, 'Could mean he'll be finnicky, want to dot every 'i' and cross every 't' too.'

They nudged their mounts down and as they reached the edge of town, two riders appeared, coming out of the shade of a large tree above a pile of boulders. They were well dressed and each carried a rifle, butt on the thigh, finger through the guard and on the trigger, thumb on the hammer spur. They wore tin stars on their shirtfronts.

They were in their thirties, Chris

judged, the bearded one older than his companion. It was the clean-shaven one who spoke.

''Mornin', gents. You got business in Kinlaw?'

'That's where we're headed,' Cade said levelly. 'Why the guns?'

'Just for appearance,' said the one with the beard, but neither Cade nor Duggan put much faith in that: these men seemed confident and ready for trouble if it reared its head. 'Like to welcome our visitors and make sure they got enough means to book into one of our hotels or rooming houses, stall their horses at the livery — generally take care of their everyday living, you know what I mean?'

'Believe I do,' Cade said nodding soberly. 'We've had a rough trail . . . '

'It shows,' said the beardless one.

'On our way to see the marshal.'

'What're your names?'

They told the deputies and the bearded man ran his gaze openly over their gun rigs and the scarred butt of

196

Cade's rifle showing above the scabbard.

'Your Winchester's had some use, but your friend don't seem to have one — just an empty scabbard.'

'Lost it, way back at the edge of the sierras.'

'Bad bushwhack country.'

The deputies waited for a reply. Chris gave it to them, voice harder now.

'We had some trouble. Fellers wanted to keep us from seeing the marshal. How about taking us to him instead of sittin' out here in the sun, and us with growlin' bellies.'

'Well, you don't seem too dangerous, but you seem like men with trouble, have to keep looking over your shoulders.'

'That's us,' spoke up Duggan. 'I'm an engineer and Chris here, is temporary sheriff of Reno Creek. *Now*, can we for Chris'sakes see the damn marshal!'

His tone didn't seem to faze the men in anyway, but the beardless one looked to the other to make a reply.

'No — ' He lifted a hand quickly as he saw the two ragged men stiffen in leather. 'Marshal Dobbs is away at present. Was a shooting up at Dodge a few weeks back and the marshal was involved. He's up there at the trial now, being a witness for the prosecution.

'Any idea when he'll be back,' asked Cade.

'Aw, a few days, I guess. I see you've moved your vest enough for me to see that sheriff's badge on your shirt pocket. What d'you mean 'temporary' sheriff?'

'They never swore me in properly. Had me sign a contract when I was still groggy comin' out of dental gas.'

That made the men glance at each other smartly.

'Judge Kirk, maybe?' asked the beardless one and Cade nodded. 'Yeah, there's been talk about the way things're kinda loose-run up there . . . You're Cade then?'

Chris nodded. 'Brick here has some information that I don't feel I could

198

authenticate well enough for it to stand up in court. That's why we want to see the US marshal, have him take Brick's deposition.'

'Yeah, well, you better come on in. Fact, there's a telegraph message waiting for you, Cade. Follow us.'

Actually, it wasn't follow 'us' — only the bearded one rode out front, his companion bringing up the rear, still with his rifle at the ready . . .

The telegraph message was addressed to 'Chris Cade, Sheriff, Reno Creek, Kansas', care of the Kinlaw Telegraph Agency.

Regret inform you Wiley condition critical. Asking for you. Return soonest.
Hawkins, MD.

While Chris and Duggan had skirted the sierra country on the way to Kinlaw, taking time to cover their trail, hide out occasionally, Crowe returned to Reno Creek at a fast clip. He went straight to Judge Kirk's office to report.

The town council was having an unofficial meeting and as well as Kirk, Burl Randall, Doc Payne, Latham the storekeeper and Madam Scarlet of the town's only 'offically-recognized' whorehouse, were present.

None of them seemed to care much for Crowe barging straight in and the judge half-rose out of his chair, then suddenly sat down again and waved a hand at the other councillors who were starting to protest.

'Didn't expect to see you so soon,' the judge said briskly.

Crowe leaned against the door, took out the makings and began to build a cigarette. 'No, thought I might's well report in.'

'I'd've thought you'd still be after Cade and Duggan, so let's hope your 'report' will be to the effect that they are both dead . . . ?'

Payne was the one to growl this and got nods from the others in silent agreement.

Crowe's match flared and he dipped the end of his cigarette into it, exhaling a plume of smoke carelessly across the table around which the others were sitting. The judge frowned as he irritably waved a hand in front of his face. 'Well? Damn you, Crowe, don't play games with us!'

Crowe heaved a sigh. 'No easy way to say it, I guess.' He ran his hard gaze around the expectant, impatient faces. 'What I found on the far slopes of the sierras ain't gonna please you . . . '

'Let us be the judge of that!' Latham snapped.

'Be my guest. The long and short of it is that they're all dead.'

There was an expectant silence and it was Kirk who asked tightly, 'Who . . . are . . . 'all'? I certainly hope it includes Cade and Duggan!'

Crowe pursed his lips, then gave a brief shake of his head. 'Sorry, judge. Far as I know they're already in Kinlaw.'

That caused a lot of comment, not

any of it complimentary to Crowe, but he leaned against the wall and took a few more drags on his cigarette until they quietened down.

'Explain!' Judge Kirk roared.

'Had a helluva time trackin' Montana's bunch in the sierras. Heard a lot of shootin', rode towards it, when I finally got there they were all dead.'

'Montana and his men, you mean?'

'That's right, Doc. Every last one of 'em.'

'And Cade and Duggan?'

'No sign, well, what I mean is, they were long gone by the looks of the tracks. By the time I buried Montana and his boys, they'd've been well along the trail to Kinlaw and I'd never've caught up with 'em before they got there.'

More consternation and Crowe simply let the wild questions stream past his ears, took a last drag on his cigarette and walked across to crush out the butt in an ashtray on Kirk's desk.

The judge's look was not friendly.

'In other words, you let them get away.'

'Didn't *let* 'em, Judge, just was no sense in me tryin' to overtake 'em when they had such a big lead.'

'If you hadn't taken time to dig graves,' Burl growled, no longer his usual friendly self, 'you could've caught 'em.'

Crowe looked uncomfortable. 'Well, mebbe, Burl. Fact is, I didn't fancy goin' up agin Cade: he'd've been the one to take care of Montana's boys — I know his reputation — but, like I said, they'd've still gotten to Kinlaw ahead of me. But there's one good thing.'

'I'd be damn well interested to know what *that* is!' snapped Madam Scarlet.

'I heard just the other day that Marshal Dobbs is up in Dodge, on some court case about a shootin'. So they won't be able to see him for a spell yet.'

His words brought a thoughtful silence to the room, but the tension was still a tangible thing.

'How long before Dobbs is due back in Kinlaw?' asked Kirk.

Crowe shrugged. 'You'd have a better idea than me, Judge, about how long such trials go on, I mean . . . '

'Aaah! There're so many things that can delay them, drag them out. It's anybody's guess.'

'Well, maybe we could get at Cade and Duggan before he gets back.'

'That's too big a chance to take!' snapped Kirk. 'Those deputies of Dobbs's are no fools.'

'We could try to get 'em back here, before the damn marshal returned to Kinlaw.'

Everyone turned to look at Burl who made this surprise suggestion, and added, quietly. 'There's that whore of mine, Wiley, who got shot . . . I know damn well Cade likes her . . . '

★   ★   ★

'Hell, that's bad luck, Chris,' Duggan said, as Chris handed him the message in the Kinlaw Telegraph Agency. 'You better go back to Reno, pronto. I'll wait for the marshal and make my deposition. What's wrong? You look doubtful.'

'Hawkins was certain sure Wiley was gonna be OK.'

'Yeah, well, you can never tell with bullet wounds.' Cade glanced at the eye-shaded operator. 'I want to send a wire to Dr Shelby Hawkins, Reno Creek, right away.'

The man grabbed a yellow pad and pencil. 'Go ahead.'

'*Sorry about Wiley. Coming. Cade.* That'll go direct to Doc Hawkins, won't it?'

The operator finished writing. 'It better. It's a federal offence to meddle with telegraphic mail. Sender and addressee only. You got reason to believe your message could be interferred with?'

'No-o, not a 'reason', just a hunch it might be.'

'Well, anyone intercepts that message and don't pass it on to Doc Hawkins, is in a heap of trouble!'

Cade nodded: 'We'll wait for a reply.'

The bearded deputy said, 'Don't need one, do you?'

'Let's see if someone thinks we do.'

The deputy nodded slowly. 'Uh-huh. See just how anxious someone is to make sure you go back to Reno, eh?'

'We can clean up and have somethin' to eat while we're hanging around, can't we?' Duggan asked.

'Better have a sawbones take a look at your hands and feet, too,' Cade said and the younger deputy went to fetch the local doctor.

★ ★ ★

When Cade's wire reached the telegraph depot at Reno Creek, Angus Biddel, the operator, hand shaking, showed the message to a hardfaced, gunhung man from Padlock, who was slouching in a chair crammed into a corner.

'I . . . I could lose my job over this.'

'Better that than your life,' the man said as he took the message form and hurried out.

He made straight for Judge Kirk's offices.

12

Return to Reno

The beardless deputy was named Hallam, and he told Chris that Doc Hawkins's original message had arrived barely forty minutes before Cade and Duggan had shown up on the town's outskirts.

This time, in reply to Chris's acceptance, the message read:

Hurry. Wiley sinking fast. Bring Duggan.
Doc Hawkins.

Chris, cleaned up, and with a fresh shirt on, glanced up and grinned crookedly at the others in the telegraph office. 'Just a mite too much enthusiasm, gents. And why would they want Brick to come? He hasn't even met Wiley.'

Duggan, spruced-up some, too, left hand bandaged after the doctor's visit, now tugged at one ear lobe with his right hand. 'We-ell, actually I did meet her one night in the Buckjumpin' Gal . . . if you know what I mean.'

Cade arched his eyebrows. 'Well, what d'you know . . . ?'

'It was strictly business,' said Duggan, gazing steadily at Cade. 'Our . . . relationship was short, and I have to say 'sweet'. But there's no reason why Hawkins would think any different and want me there now.'

'Someone thinks there is,' Cade corrected him.

Duggan waved a hand curtly. 'Yeah, but sounds to me like *someone* just wants to make sure we *both* go back. This was what you were hoping for, Chris? That they got too confident, stressed it just that little bit too much.'

Chris nodded, frowning slightly. 'At the same time, seems kind of a stupid mistake for Judge Kirk to make if he is the one sendin' messages in Doc

Hawkins's name. I gave Kirk credit for more brains, but . . . ' He spread his arms.

'Well, someone did it, Chris. Anyway, I want to go back.'

Cade turned to Varney, the bearded deputy. 'Can we get fresh horses? A rifle for Brick, some ammo . . . ?'

'Yeah, we can fix that, but I reckon Duggan better write out his deposition and sign it in front of me and Hal before he goes. We can have Marshal Dobbs check it over when he comes back. That way, we'll at least know what the hell's going on.'

'Good idea,' Duggan said. 'I can give you the location of that arroyo I found blocked, and — '

Varney held up a hand. 'Dunno what you're talkin' about right now. Just write it down and we'll see you're outfitted properly. One of us could trail you, just in case, if you wanted . . . ?'

Chris shook his head. 'Thanks, no. I think we'll be met along the way.'

'Yeah,' Hallam said flatly. 'Maybe by

a slug in the back.'

'We'll keep our eyes open,' Cade assured him. 'We'll be ready.'

Brick Duggan didn't seem too reassured. But he didn't retract his offer to ride along with Cade, either.

⋆ ⋆ ⋆

They figured to take a different trail back to Reno Creek than the one that had brought them down here. So Hallam and Varney unrolled a large-scale county map, had a slight argument about which way would be best, then compromised and found that the different trails they had chosen eventually linked up into one that would lead the travellers into the area both had had in mind.

For hard-eyed, dead-serious deputy lawmen, they both had the grace to look somewhat sheepish when they realized they'd been arguing for no purpose.

'Sorry for that, fellers,' Varney said, unbending enough to almost smile.

'Dobbs let's us act more or less independently most times, so we have the odd difference of opinion.'

'Long as we get back to Reno away from the trail we took comin' down. I have an idea there might be some more fellers we'd rather not meet waiting along it,' said Chris, and the deputies agreed.

Duggan didn't have much to say during this discussion, but licked his lips frequently.

When they cleared town, mid afternoon, and against the advice of Hallam who wanted them to stay overnight, now it was so late, Cade and Duggan figured to cold-camp at a place Varney had pointed out on his map, called Cameron's Leap — no one knew why. It provided good cover, hidden from any trail that would be used over that section, as long as they weren't foolish enough to light a camp-fire . . .

They weren't, but as they washed their hardtack down with canteen water, Duggan looked around constantly as the sounds of the night started up: crickets, buzzing insects, slither noises in the brush, lizards running over rocks, the distant scream of some nightbird . . .

He lowered the canteen slowly as he dimly made out Cade's face, turned towards him. When he spoke, he sounded a little embarrassed.

'Hell! I'm not usually this jumpy, even walking into a partly-collapsed mine tunnel with a thousand tons of rock hanging over my head, ready to fall if I sneezed.'

'I don't think you're scared so much as . . . cautious. Maybe nervous. But that's understandable — this ain't the kinda situation you're used to. I'd be all froze up if I was in that tunnel you just mentioned.'

'Mmmm — maybe.'

'You've done good so far, Brick. You're willing to fight and you've pulled your weight.

Brick frowned, even though he knew

Cade couldn't see his face in detail. 'You sound like you're ex-army — officer?'

Chris shook his head. 'Hell, no. Non-com. Top Sergeant . . . Long time ago. Prefer trail drivin', though you meet the same dangers lots of times — Indians, outlaws tryin' to steal the cattle, floods, prairie fires, not all that different. But a man's his own boss on the trail, up to him what he does, whether it's right or wrong.'

'Independent. Yeah, I can figure that. Deals come up in my job where I've got to act fast or get clobbered, maybe killed if I don't make the right decision. Afterwards, if it turns out OK, you get a real good feeling, or I do.'

'Me, too. Why I never went for a commission.'

Duggan chuckled. 'Beats taking orders that, if they do go wrong, you have to take the blame as well. This way, you've only got yourself to blame.' He drank from the canteen again. 'That judge must be kicking himself, thinking he had you over a barrel and could make you jump through hoops.'

'Don't reckon I made him, or his councillors, very happy.'

'Me, either — for different reasons, of course. They must figure they're kind of jinxed by now.'

'They won't take it lyin' down as you've likely already figured. I'll take first guard, wake you in three, four hours. You do the same for me and we'll be on our way before full sunup. OK?'

Duggan stifled a yawn. 'You're the boss, boss.'

★   ★   ★

It was cold in the pre-dawn shadow cast by the sierras and darker than Cade had figured on. But they had good mounts that found a way down into the pass between the hills.

By the time sunlight washed down the slopes like a pale yellow tide, they were beginning to climb out of the pass, shivering a little.

'Be glad to hit that full sunshine up top,' opined Duggan. 'I'm not a man for cold country, dodge those assignments when I can.'

Cade was about to say something the same when he reined down suddenly, sliding his rifle out of the scabbard.

Duggan couldn't see why right away but followed suit, unsheathed his borrowed Winchester, fumbling a little with his bandaged hand.

By then Chris had jacked a load into the action, holding the rifle in both hands now, ready to shoot.

Then Duggan saw the rider sitting his horse in the middle of the narrow trail at the top of the steep rise, his rifle butt resting on one thigh. Duggan squinted.

'Who the hell's that?' There was a faint tension in his voice. Then he stiffened, started to lift out of the saddle as he frowned. 'Say, he used to come out to Magruder's now and again. He works for Judge Kirk!'

Chris nodded slowly, not taking his

eyes off the man blocking their way.

'Yeah, calls himself Crowe . . . with an 'e'.'

'Keep comin', Sheriff!' Crowe called, swinging the rifle to his shoulder. They were too far away to hear the hammer cock but Cade knew it was all the way back, ready to fall with the pressure of Crowe's thick finger on the trigger. 'You make a fine target agin all that pale rock below you!'

Cade remained still. Duggan seemed uncertain what to do.

'See you got my wire, bringin' Duggan, too.'

'*Your* wire?' Chris sounded surprised. 'Thought it was the judge sendin' 'em.'

'Yeah, I just kind of added that bit about bringin' Duggan . . . Thought it might tip you off it was a fake.'

The engineer looked puzzledly at Cade. 'What's he talking about?'

'Seems *he* wanted you to come back to Reno with me. But looks like this is about as far as we go.'

'Judas Priest! You . . . you think he's gonna shoot us down in cold blood?'

'Looks like it. He's manoeuvred us to where he wants us. All he's gotta do is squeeze the trigger.'

'Well, I ain't sitting still for that!' Duggan's voice quavered a little but he kicked his spurs into his horse's flanks and yelled into its ear.

It lunged forward, weary though it was, and Crowe's rifle whiplashed, and again. The first slug kicked gravel between the grey's forefeet and set it shying and whinnying. Duggan fought to stay seated, his gun forgotten, handicapped by his bandaged hand. He started to fall as the second bullet drew a spurt of dust from Cade's bedroll.

The smoke's rear end swerved and Cade quickly clamped his knees and tightened his grip on the reins, instinctive movements, bare seconds, but occupying him so that his rifle was ignored for that time.

The third shot smacked into the

ground beside Duggan where he lay spreadeagled from his fall. As Chris got his gelding settled and finally started to bring his rifle up, Crowe called, confidently.

'Them's the warnin' shots. Next one's the first of the killer bullets with your names on 'em. You gonna use the rifle, Sheriff . . . ? Up to you, but I'd rather you leathered it.'

Chris frowned. Sounded like Crowe wanted to *palaver — or was it only to gloat . . . ?*

He took a chance — pushed the rifle back into the scabbard and lifted his hands out to the side.

'Now that's right accommodatin' of you. Hey, Duggan. You gonna lie there all day? On your feet and stand beside Cade. Your bronc won't run far.'

Duggan did as he was told, frowning up at Chris who shrugged his shoulders.

'He gonna kill us anyway?' he asked hoarsely.

Keeping his gaze on Crowe as the

man walked his mount carefully down the steep slope, Chris said, thoughtfully,

'Anybody's guess.'

13

The Captain

Crowe made them dismount and sit in a cramped area between two boulders. He didn't take their six-guns but that really didn't matter because, while it was possible to roll a cigarette, they couldn't move their arms with enough freedom to slide the Colts out of leather.

Crowe seemed relaxed, but there was that dangerous wariness in his eyes that Chris recalled from way back up on the Wind River in his soldiering days.

Crowe sat easily on a rounded boulder, built a cigarette with his rifle no more than four inches from his hand, lit it with a vesta struck on his left thumbnail, the rifle by then held, cocked, in his right hand.

Exhaling, he almost grinned. 'Sorry

lookin' pair as I ever did see! Hell, din' you figure someone'd be watchin' the trails back to Reno?'

'Sure. See how unlucky we were, pickin' the one you were guarding.'

Crowe shook his head slowly. 'Not by chance. I know this damn country almost as well as I know the parade ground at Fort McLaren.' He paused and grinned again at the startled look on the faces of his prisoners. Yeah, it's *Captain* Crowe, boys! Staff of General Hartmann.'

He set his gaze on Cade's face and Chris frowned. '*General* Hartmann . . . ? I recall a Major Paul Hartmann . . . '

'You been away for a long time, Cade. Yeah, he's general now, got a big staff. I'm one. And when that wagon of gold our troop was responsible for gettin' safely to Dodge just up and disappeared, well, our general wasn't happy . . . ' He *tut-tutted*. 'No blots on the general's book, see . . . ? Tore this country apart lookin' for that wagon. Wore out team after team, sifted through every little clue. Finally, nailed it down to this county, though he figured the hold-up and massacre happened a good ways from here.'

Cade rolled a cigarette and lit it, handing it to Duggan, then rolled himself one. 'So you're his hotshot?'

Crowe shrugged. 'I do all right — had an incentive. The lieutenant in charge of that wagon party was my kid brother.' His voice was steel-edged and his jaw jutted involuntarily. 'I asked for a year's leave to try and solve the whole thing and Hartmann gave it to me. My time was up a couple months back, but he ain't sent for me yet and he won't, when I tell him I'm about home on this one.'

'You got evidence or enough clues to point at Judge Kirk and his cronies?' Cade asked and didn't like the bleak look Crowe threw him for leaping ahead of his story.

'Yeah! He had a gunslinger body-guard named Tate — you likely heard of him? 'Cracker' Tate?' Cade nodded but

Duggan shook his head. 'I kinda got him riled in Burl Randall's saloon one time and we went for our guns.'

He broke off: no need to explain further: *he* took Tate's place as Kirk's gunslinger.

'Didn't the judge connect your name with the leader of the wagon team?' Duggan asked.

Crowe smiled crookedly. 'Kid was underage when he run off and joined the army, used the name 'Byrd', see?'

'Yeah. 'Bird — Crow'. So you went to work for Judge Kirk, and . . . ?' Cade urged somewhat impatiently.

'Been gatherin' what evidence I can, but I need to be able to prove Kirk's bunch are behind it all. Then Duggan turned up and his survey results threw the judge and his pards into a screamin' blue fit. The river he wanted to divert would run into the very damn arroyo where they'd buried the wagon.'

'And the soldiers they'd killed,' added Chris.

Crowe's face was bleaker and more

ugly than usual as he nodded tightly. 'I could never find out just where that damn arroyo was! I tried everythin' to pump the council, broke into their desks — no good! Then they tried to kill Duggan and Magruder whipped him outta sight when it went wrong and Mel Hawkins got stomped. Thought at the time they'd finally killed Duggan by then and hid the body. Then you showed, Cade. They figured that havin' a lawman under their control, well, you can guess how smug the bastards were feelin'.'

'It was you shot up those men when we were travelling down to Kinlaw?' Duggan asked and Crowe nodded jerkily.

'Yeah, and then they figured you hadn't got to see Marshal Dobbs because he was away, and Burl Randall thought up the telegraph idea about Wiley dyin', just to get you to come back before Dobbs returned to Dodge — and you'd be ambushed along the trail.'

'How is Wiley?' Cade cut in tensely. 'She's not really . . . dyin' is she?'

Crowe looked steadily at him, then shook his head. 'Nah, far as I know she's all right. But you *thinkin'* that she was dyin', brought you runnin'.'

'I had to be sure. So, you're clever as a professor and lured us here. Now what?'

Crowe shifted his gaze to Duggan. 'I want him to take me to where the wagon's buried.'

Duggan stiffened. 'What makes you think I know . . . ?'

'What you found threw Kirk and his friends into a somersault. So you know, all right.' He swung the rifle around suddenly, cocking the hammer. 'Or, put it this way, you *better* know.'

Cade remained quiet, seeing Duggan was thinking hard. Then he sighed and nodded. 'All I know is I found an arroyo that'd had part of the hillock above blasted down into it. The river I had in mind to divert would run right through that area, probably wash away that mound of dirt.'

'And expose the wagon!' Crowe snapped, eyes glinting. 'Yeah! That's what I thought was goosin' 'em!'

'I have no real proof it's there, Crowe.'

'You take me to that arroyo! I'll dig if it breaks my spine, but I bet I'll find that wagon, and what's left of Lonnie . . . That's all I need.'

'You won't have any proof it was Kirk and company who did the robbery,' Cade pointed out quietly.

'No? Happens I know a feller named Sven Larsen — used to blacksmith in Reno, but he's a lunger, had to move to a drier country. He's in a sanitorium in Nevada now. Told me he could only afford it because Judge Kirk paid him a heap of money to melt down some gold — din' say where he got it — and cast it into rough rods that could be broken into pieces and look like nuggets dug outta the ground . . . easy to cash, see?' He looked from one to the other. 'How does that sound?'

'OK,' Chris said. 'If Larsen'll tell it to the law.'

'He will. He ain't doin' so good and if he thinks he's gonna die, he'll want to unload his conscience. He's got religion since he took so bad.'

'They wouldn't've buried the gold with the wagon.'

Crowe smiled crookedly. 'I know that, I got off a coupla wires, too. Them Reno councillors won't get far if they run. Good ol' Gen'ral Hartmann'll have troopers watchin' every trail between here and Dodge.'

Chris looked towards Duggan, surprised to see the man looking so worried. 'Brick . . . ?'

Duggan said slowly. 'There's one other thing about this arroyo where the mound is: it's on Magruder's land.'

*　*　*

Crowe knew a way around the Padlock home range that would take them to the arroyo without being seen by Magruder.

They rode far and hard, sat out

228

another uncomfortable night under a ledge with more rain gusting in on them through the dark hours. Cade and Duggan huddled in their blankets and slickers but Crowe, who only had his range clothes, sat soaking wet and, Chris reckoned, awake, most of the night.

No doubt the building tension and excitement were enough to destroy any real thought of sleep.

They chewed jerky and washed the spicy lumps down with fresh sweet-tasting rainwater trickling over the rock of the sheltering ledge, by way of breakfast.

'C'mon! Let's go,' Crowe said, restless, eyes ablaze.

They hurried, seeing he was so wakeful. Duggan, leading his mount, picked a way down into the broken country below. Viewed from above it was like a lot of wriggling snakes, the arroyos and gulches twisting and turning in the directions ancient water-courses had carved through there.

Duggan paused several times and the sun was well up, their damp clothes steaming, when he came to the deep-sided arroyo he was looking for.

'This is the place. See where the earth slid . . . ?'

Crowe pushed to the fore, looking at the angled pile of rubble, now freshly runnelled from the rain overnight. It sloped up out of the gully to a side of the hillock where tons of dirt and rock had obviously broken away — or been blasted loose.

Crowe growled at Duggan who was showing signs of fatigue. There was fresh blood on the bandage around his injured fingers, too, as he sat down wearily on a rock. Crowe yanked him roughly to his feet. 'Show me!'

'Easy, Crowe,' Cade told him. 'We're here, man. Relax.'

'I got a spare spade! Grab it and lend a hand.'

Chris had no trouble with that and Duggan scouted around, indicated an area almost up against the opposite wall.

'I had an impression of something arched, there. Nothing showing, but the shape could've been part of a wheel if you use your imagination.'

'Why the hell didn't you look?' growled Crowe, starting to dig with his short-handled spade into the mud.

'One of Magruder's riders saw me, took me in at gunpoint, thought I was a trespasser. Look, that doesn't matter. But here's where I reckon we should start.'

Chris stepped closer and began to spade up mud, noticing there was dry earth only a couple of inches down. The rain had stopped and apparently hadn't soaked in very deeply.

'Let's see what we can find . . . '

While Crowe and Cade kept digging, Duggan wandered down the twisting arroyo, kicking a rock here, a clod of earth there. He didn't realize he had moved out from the shelter of the highest walls of the arroyo and was visible from the waist up now. He also didn't realize he hadn't ground-hitched his horse; it was a Padlock animal and now wandered back across its home range, looking for company.

It found another horse, but there was a rider on it and the man leaned down, picked up the trailing reins and rode back towards the chuckwagon of the roundup camp just over the knoll.

'Boss!' he called to Magruder who was arguing with the cook over the standard of the food he was serving up to his crew. The rancher looked up irritably, saw the rider and the dappled grey horse he was leading.

'Where the hell did that come from? It's one Mustang had in the remuda up at the linecamp . . . '

'Well, it was wanderin' out near them old gulches you told us to keep the cows out of. I was lookin' for a stray when I seen it. But I found this in the saddle-bags.' The rider held up the brass sight from Duggan's theodolite.

Magruder strode forward, snatched it from the man's hand. He twisted it and found some engraving on the barrel:

B.J. Duggan — 1874.

He snapped his head up, looked quickly towards the gulch country.

'Get a few of the boys!' he said in a tight voice. 'And tell 'em to make sure their guns're loaded!'

★   ★   ★

'Aw, Christ!'

Cade looked up swiftly as Crowe exclaimed and Duggan, starting to climb up the steep-sided wall, stopped so suddenly he slipped and skidded down almost at Crowe's feet.

The man was pulling something out of the mud. It looked like rotting cloth, but something glinted dully on it and fell with a small plop. Crowe snatched it up and showed it to the others as they came closer.

It was a button off an army tunic.

'Well,' Crowe said, taking a deep breath. 'I guess this is . . . what I was lookin' for all along.'

Cade handed the button back to

Crowe. 'If you like, I'll dig some more just there.'

Crowe's face straightened. 'Like hell! *We'll* dig! And the sooner the better!'

He pushed Chris aside and began deep, wide-swinging motions with the spade, spattering the others with mud.

Chris and Duggan exchanged glances.

'There won't be a . . . a lot left that you'd recognize . . . after all this time, Crowe,' Duggan said haltingly.

Crowe didn't even pause. 'I'll recognize Lonnie, unless the bastards took his class graduation ring!'

He was snorting, breathless with emotion more than the physical labour. Chris nodded to Duggan to stay clear and began to dig a few feet away. Almost at once, the shovel blade clanged on the rusted iron rim of a wagonwheel . . .

The next clang came from a bullet tearing the spade from Cade's hands. Without pause he dropped flat, slid down the slope of the small mound where they had been working, palming up his six-gun.

Even as he slid and rolled he saw the men on foot coming over the edge of the arroyo and recognized Magruder at once. More bullets *thunked!* into the mud as he hurled himself aside, shooting and yelling at Duggan to get down.

The engineer had trouble getting his Colt free and Cade swore as he saw the big man shudder, step back a pace and then drop to one knee. Guns blazed along the rim again and Brick Duggan twisted to the side, falling against a bank of sodden dirt and sliding off to roll on to his face.

Crowe was on one knee, working his rifle, bullets spitting gravel and mud from the arroyo's edge. Cade saw a man's hat fly off, the owner jerking to his feet, head thrown back, face all bloody.

Then Crowe ran forward, yelling, rifle butt braced against his hip, working lever and trigger at a phenomonal rate. Chris drove up to a crouch, ran for the cover of a rock, lead spattering mud and grit around his pounding boots.

He hurled himself bodily behind the rock as two bullets screamed off in snarling ricochets. He rolled on to his back, punched out used cartridges and thumbed home new ones, dropping two in his haste. His rock was peppered with lead and he saw Crowe was down on one knee, sagging, rifle in the mud, but he was still groping for his six-gun.

Chris lurched upright as two men directed their fire at Crowe. He fanned off three shots, more for distraction than any real hope of finding a target. But one slug seared into the man beside Magruder and, as the cowboy fell, the wiry rancher bared his teeth, clamped his left hand around his right wrist and beaded Chris's running figure.

Cade dropped, rolled on to his side, and, gun angled upwards, emptied it into Pat Magruder. The rancher, lifted off his feet by the hammering lead, fell face down into a puddle that covered him to the ears. There were no air bubbles after the first splash . . .

Gasping, Cade looked around. Two cowboys who had accompanied Magruder were running for their horses down the gulch: they had no intention of continuing the fight. Duggan was unmoving and, tight-lipped, Chris hurried across.

He turned Brick on to his back and swore even as he grimaced: half the engineer's face had been blown away . . .

There was a shadow suddenly blotting out the sun and he looked up quickly, remembering he was holding an empty gun.

It was Crowe, blood running down one side of his face.

'Thought you were dead,' Cade said flatly.

'I ain't that easy to kill. Scalp crease, knocked me out for a minute. Well, we got what we wanted. Might's well go on in and upset the Judge.'

'We take Duggan with us for decent burial.'

Crowe looked at Chris's hard face and shrugged. 'He was your friend,' he said and turned away, holding a grubby kerchief to the scalp crease.

* * *

First stop after leaving Duggan at the undertaker's, was the infirmary. Chris was pleasantly surprised at the way his heart seemed to leap when he saw Wiley sitting up in bed, drinking a cup of coffee.

She was startled to see him and smiled warmly as he came across. 'You look like hell, if you don't mind me saying so.'

'You don't, you look . . . look . . . real damn good!' He quickly told her about the telegraph messages he had received and she looked at him soberly.

'You were going to come back . . . because you thought I was . . . dying . . . ?'

He nodded. 'Glad the wires were fake.'

Her hand found his and she squeezed.

238

There were tears brimming in her eyes. 'Sorry,' she said huskily. 'Us . . . whores ain't much used to someone really caring about us.'

'Well, I just thought of you as a good-lookin' woman who saved my life.'

She sniffled, dabbed at her eyes with a lace kerchief. 'What happens now?' she asked after he had told her briefly about recent events. 'Will you stay on as sheriff?'

'Reckon not. Think I'll go up to Dodge, see if I can pick up with a trail crew goin' back to Texas. Ride with 'em and mebbe find another herd to bring back up.'

'I — I was offered a job at the Sky-Hi saloon in Dodge. If I get it, when you bring back a herd you can look me up. You think I could ride along with you as far as Dodge now to find out if the job's still going?'

He smiled. 'Be glad of your company.'

'Can you wait around till I'm feeling

up to travelling and . . . things?'

'I guess so. We've gotta go see the judge yet.'

She sobered fast. 'You be damn careful of that two-faced snake, Chris! I mean it. He's killed men before or had them killed.'

'I'll be careful. Anyway, Crowe's coming with me. Doc Hawkins is fixing up a bullet crease on his scalp right now.'

'Couldn't you sort of let Crowe handle things?'

Soberly, he held her gaze and shook his head slowly.

'No. I shouldn't've even asked that of a man like you. But, please, Chris! Heed what I say! Kirk's a very dangerous man! He may be old and fat, but — '

'I'll be back — and I'll bring you a bunch of flowers.'

This time the tears streamed down her face unashamedly as he went out.

★　★　★

The judge was alone when they went to his offices. 'You interfering bastards! You — you've ruined all my plans!' he yelled at them hoarsely.

Chris stood by the door and Crowe, head neatly bandaged, hat pushed back, stood in front of the big, cluttered desk. 'Figured you'd've had lots of company, Judge.'

Judge Kirk swore, leaving himself breathless. 'Huh! You've never seen such a — a bunch of yellow-livered cowards once the word came you were back, Crowe. I, of course, had learned how you had duped me all this time by then! Someone found Montana and a bunch of dead men scattered across that mountain trail after you telling me you had stopped to bury them! Anyway, the rats have deserted me, walked out on their businesses, intent only on saving their worthless hides.'

'But you waited,' Cade said and the judge lifted his bleak gaze to the man he had tried to bend to his will.

'For a very good reason! You made a

fool of me, Cade, and I'm almost willing to forego my share in that gold just for the pleasure of putting a bullet in you!'

He reared to his feet, his right hand coming out from under his coat with a pepperpot hideaway gun, swinging the cluster of five barrels towards Cade who dived for the floor, sliding his Colt from leather.

It wasn't necessary.

Crowe drew and shot the judge three times in his thick body, walked over to the man as he lay bleeding and dying beside the desk and put a fourth bullet into him.

'That one was for me; the others were for Lonnie.'

Chris stood slowly, holstering his gun, but keeping his hand on the butt. 'Thanks, Crowe.'

The big, ugly man grinned tautly.

'Now you owe me.'

Cade nodded, but frowned at the look on Crowe's face. 'What . . . ?'

'We never did get paired-off for a

bare-knuckle go-round.'

Cade stared. 'What ... ? You and me? After all this time! Hell, we're both well past the days of twenty-plus round fights, Crowe.'

'Speak for yourself.'

Chris could see he was determined and finally asked, 'What d'you think your chances are of winning?'

Crowe gave it some serious thought, answered reluctantly, but honestly. ''Bout fifty-fifty, I guess. How about you.'

Chris nodded. 'The same.'

'Ought to be interestin' then, a real good, blood-splashin' go-round. You game?'

'Well, not right now.'

'No, but I got a hard head. Won't be long before this crease is healed enough.' He hesitated, then thrust out a big hand. 'Shake on it?'

Chris also hesitated a moment, then nodded and they gripped hands.

Now there was no backing down possible for either of them.

★　★　★

It was a memorable fight when it was staged a week or so later and two bloody, exhausted figures had to be prised apart after twenty-three rounds, staggering, leaning on each other for support, leaden arms dangling.

There were two referees and they agreed it had to be a draw.

Words slurred and almost unintelligible, Crowe said, 'I . . . wanna . . . re-match . . . '

Cade groaned. 'Judas wept! Don't you ever give up?'

Crowe shook his head.

'When?'

Chris threw up his aching arms.

'Aw, *hell*! he breathed fervently . . .

* * *

They still talk about *that* fight up Reno Creek way.

It became one of the legends of the cattle trails. No one is sure to this day just who the winner was.

Or even if there was one.

We do hope that you have enjoyed reading this large print book.

Did you know that all of our titles are available for purchase?

We publish a wide range of high quality large print books including:
Romances, Mysteries, Classics
General Fiction
Non Fiction and Westerns

Special interest titles available in large print are:
The Little Oxford Dictionary
Music Book, Song Book
Hymn Book, Service Book

Also available from us courtesy of Oxford University Press:
Young Readers' Dictionary
(large print edition)
Young Readers' Thesaurus
(large print edition)

For further information or a free brochure, please contact us at:
Ulverscroft Large Print Books Ltd.,
The Green, Bradgate Road, Anstey,
Leicester, LE7 7FU, England.
Tel: (00 44) **0116 236 4325**
Fax: (00 44) **0116 234 0205**

Other titles in the
Linford Western Library:

COMANCHERO TRAIL

Jack Dakota

For the new hired gun at the Rafter W, the owner's wilful granddaughter, Miss Trashy, is the first of his troubles. Dean Kittredge must then face El Serpiente and his gang of Comanchero outlaws, backed by Jensen Crudace, the land and cattle agent who plans to control the territory. Kittredge and ranch foreman Tad Sherman track down El Serpiente to his hidden base in the heart of a distant mesa. Will they succeed in stopping the ruthless gunmen?

SOFT SOAP FOR A HARD CASE

Billy Hall

Sam Heller had been hit — hampered in his speed of drawing and holding a gun. He and a homesteader faced Lance Russell and his trusty sidekick when they stepped out from behind a shed. Two against two, yet Sam didn't have a chance: he would always struggle to outdraw them. Meanwhile, Kate Bond waited, hoping for his return, whilst her beloved Sam was determined to go down fighting. Then Russell and his hired gunmen went for their guns . . .

THE MARK OF TRASK

Michael D. George

Mohawk Flats was a peaceful town in a fertile valley; its townsfolk had never required weaponry. They'd grown wealthy and naïve regarding the ways of the outside world — until the ruthless Largo gang arrived. They discovered an Eden ripe and ready for the taking, unaware that a famed gunfighter, Trask, was hot on their trail. Although ill, he knew what had to be done. Soon the Largo gang would know why Trask was feared by all who faced him . . .

KATO'S ARMY

D. M. Harrison

Wells Fargo Agent Jay Kato didn't want to deliver this consignment of gold. Green River Springs held too many bad memories and his cousin, Duke Heeley, threatened to kill him if he ever returned there. However, misgivings were put aside with the offer of a generous bonus, just to deliver the money to the marshal. But as he stepped off the train, a hail of bullets greeted him. Kato would have to raise an army to fight them all.

THE PRAIRIE MAN

I. J. Parnham

When young friends Temple Kennedy and Hank Pierce, ignored ghostly warnings about the 'Prairie Man' and continued with their daring, nightly adventures, it almost led to a tragic accident. But Hank had saved his friend's life and Temple vowed to return the favour. Fifteen years later, Hank, a respected citizen, is wrongly accused of murder. Temple, now an outlaw, vows to save Hank. However, his investigations lead to a man who isn't even supposed to exist: the Prairie Man . . .